Claude Pélieu
Kali Yug Express

Translated by
Mary Beach

Foreword by
Charles Plymell

Bottle of Smoke Press

Special thanks to Benoît Delaune and Pierre Joris for
their advice during the translation and editing process.

The publisher would like to thank Byron Coley,
Thurston Moore & James Grauerholz for helping make
this project happen.

ISBN-13:   978-1-937073-03-9

Bottle of Smoke Press
902 Wilson Drive
Dover, DE 19904
www.bospress.net

New Kind of Fascism has emerged in the wake of the so-called acid-revolution. Born of boredom, loneliness and intense spiritual hunger, it has captured some of America's most creative young minds.—In a period of extreme personal liberation, it has caused more and more believers to opt for servility, to let their lives & their careers, pleasures, loyalties, even choice of lovers—& be controlled by the holy whim of one man.

David Felton. From Mindfuckers, Straight Arrow Books, 1972

claude
PELIEU

kali yug
express

CHRISTIAN BOURGOIS ÉDITEUR

FOR CHARLES PLYMELL

IN MEMORIAM LEE CRABTREE

Claude Pélieu
KALI YUG EXPRESS

Peter Engstler Verlag

FOREWORD

The British scientist, Rupert Sheldrake, wrote about Morphic Resonance, positing that morphogenetic fields impose influences on otherwise random patterns of activity that keep natural laws emerging. For instance one species in an altogether different part of the globe creates the same activity as another at the same time, though there is no direct connection. This has been evident in the creative forces of history. In Joyce's day, a more direct evolution, metempsychosis, one artist dies and his creative powers are born in another. Some have noticed through the ages that periods in art and literature are related in ways independent of an individual's creative intercourse.

Over the last half century we "saw thy change begin" to quote Hart Crane. The Sixties were a time of change. Jackson Pollack had randomly created signature works by chance and kinetic energy. Chaos Theory had helped Duchamp's nude up the staircase. John Cage made every note a democratic noise that defined harmonies to larger ears. Fibonacci, phyllotaxis and fractals caught up in the same speed of hype and cutups juxtaposed hypocrisies brought new futurisms while spilling heavy metal back into the naive "revolushuns." The stage was ready for Claude Pélieu, linear descendant of Céline, Artaud, Baudelaire armed with his misanthropic disgust with the human species and his style, hype found in everyday speech filled with double entendre ornaments became the fretwork of their own profundities. Céline inspired him daily at his words, at his collage: "Life is filigree work. What is

7

written clearly is not worth much, it's the transparency that counts." One sees the true fate of Joe Verminex struggling between the lines for meaning, momentarily free from control through pitiful chance and accidental juxtaposition. This book is a "collage novel;" there is no genre for it. Stylistically, it is heightened prose, closest to Rimbaud and Burroughs. The French call it "texts" so it's a text with cosmic characters. It's visionary and prophetic.

It was an in-between period after the Sixties that didn't change the world, and its "revolutionaries" who brought us Baby Boomers with their 401Ks, the Kingdom of The Flower age brought us Electronic Democracy, the "devaluation of human stock" as Burroughs would have it with the same old mobsters in control . . . shameful invasions of other countries murdering collateral innocents, killing and maiming our young. Goya's "Saturn eating his children," propaganda so complete in politically correct lies that the youth slouching into death couldn't understand why they were sacrificed. Eisenhower's warning ignored. Populations depleting the landscape. Catastrophic climate changes. Haiti becomes the microcosm of Empires "Hamburger planet cracks and breaks the windows—neon waves its black flag—my hurricane-lamp looks nice . . . I'm there here, I was there, elsewhere nowhere . . . Maryland, New York, Los Angeles, San Fran, London, Paris, who cares? . . . infinity doesn't cause death to overflow." The Titanic sinks slowly in the racial consciousness.

Like Hart Crane and the Surrealist hoboes of earlier

times, "possessed, resigned." The Cosmic Conductor looks at his pocket watch *"Time's rendings, time's blendings they construe/As final reckonings of fire and snow; Strange bird-wit, like the elemental gist/Of unwalled winds they offer, singing low . . ."* The next generation calls on board those artists who don't need the academe, who don't drink from the mainstream. They created their own resonance while inhaling the perfume of Descartes' Invisible Rose. Pélieu and his cronies Jégou, Hubaut, Burroughs, Flémal, Nuttall, Weissner can . . . kept riding that Visionary Express, their table at the window while seeing this world go by in an instant or eternity we hear him say *"—we live with or without masks, on the fringe of institutions, and we sometimes speak beside nature, near reality– but nevertheless we speak a 'social language' in the heart of explosions of violence, dominated by our own –media– by our own myths, we speak–our–time, laminated by the most repressive structures. We're suffocating. It's 'this & that' say some—let's send them back into the old suffocating film—the control machine has become more and more discrete and efficient."*

Pélieu had experienced war and all the despicable traits that humans could bring upon each other, mentally and physically and then some. A new "style" in literature was certainly needed. Words became cumbersome, and couldn't keep up with the needed language in literature that jumped beyond the bop prosody that Kerouac put middle class kids to bed reading.

"Claude Pélieu and I have exchanged letters and manuscripts for some

9

years. I am frequently struck by
precise though seemingly coincidental
references in his work to what I am
writing right now writing which
nobody but myself has directly seen. I
feel that we are sharing a common
source of literary material and a
common source of thought that
perhaps all serious writers are in a very
real sense so united. By serious writers
I mean those who have left the concept
of art for art's sake behind and see
writing as a weapon with revolvers
aimed voici le temps de l'assassin."
William Burroughs

By 1968, "a new consciousness was affirming itself . . ."
riots were breaking out in the major cities of the world.
My wife, Pam Beach, and I saw Claude Pélieu and
Mary Beach in the rubble of the cobblestone streets of
Paris and then went on to London to visit William
Burroughs on Duke St. whose comments used about
Kali Yug Express and the two writers/artist, in general
confirmed the notion of the resonating activity taking
place in the Cosmos at the time. Like Burroughs, in
Naked Lunch, Pélieu used mythic characters to carry
the work like traditional "novels" of literature, but I
would call it "collage text" or a collage novel to serve
literary credence. Jeff Nuttall in *Bomb Culture*
(Delacorte Press, 1968):

> *"By 1964 a new generation had arrived*
> *in San Francisco and made City Lights*

their rendezvous. Claude Pélieu, a young Frenchman with a thorough understanding of surrealism, had arrived with Mary Beach, the daughter [sic] of Joyce's publisher. Both were aware of the fact that cutup was an adventure which extended on the one hand psychic adventure of surrealist automatic writing and on the other hand the purely aesthetic juxtaposition of language fragments begun by Pound and the imagists. Friends and cooperatives of Pélieu were Charles Plymell, a jazzy poet from Kansas, one time editor of Now Now, who did sadistic collages . . . the two Bulletins from Nowhere and Grist from Wichita give the prevailing mood.

Both writers would become prominent visual artists to complement their word. Pélieu changed the images around him daily with collage. Burroughs later used the velocity of bullets to amplify his changing images. He told me that to make art is simply easier than writing. *Kali Yug* is a visionary, prophetic book, written when the Hippies and Yippies were dissolving the Sixties, which didn't give us the political and social change needed; instead their antics at Chicago gave us more, more Nixon and those to come who ignored Eisenhower's warning of the Military Industrial Complex. Pélieu saw Céline's words become the reality: "The poetry of heroism appeals irresistibly to those who don't go to war, and even more so to those

11

who the war is making enormously wealthy."

In Montreal as in San Francisco though the counter culture enlisted, in Nuttall's words:" . . . the wild me of the fifties had taken on an almost grandfatherly air." In 1975 after the publication of *Kali Yug* at the Montreal conference "rien contre ça" featuring Claude Pélieu, Jean-Louis Brau, Charles Plymell, William Burroughs, Allen Ginsberg, Mary Beach and others, the Situationist Party, which Pélieu understood, had already perceived the futuristic virus and didn't seem to have the relevance for the Québecois who had their own "revolutionary agenda" different than the 60s hippies and yippies but not quite ready for Pélieu. This wasn't the Beatle invasion and to punctuate what the cosmic revolutionaries had experienced as control, just step over the line at Kent State.

The reality of the situation was seen by those who had a larger picture as the continuation of the Big Scam. Burroughs and Pélieu would see that "control" comes from something that is inherent to daily life, wars, social activities. And the universal dumbing down of the Prussian education system that wants to turn out good workers, good soldiers, good clerks of industry and the state know best how Saturn devours his children. There was something more to the generations of Orwell's kids who had become hip while smoking in the boy's room out of range for the Big Control's voice. To paraphrase Céline: "We've no use for intellectuals in this outfit." They need more squares, more chumps, more chimps, more proles who will not question authority. They certainly don't want ideas, ideals or visions or signs of real life. "We will think for you, my friend. Don't forget it", to which Pélieu would add: "And you, pygmies, arrive too late, with old addresses and bad vibrations."

But he would retain jazz to his last breath. Many times, he would drive people crazy turning up jazz and digging it like in the 50s. He was happy to find someone of that era, who flipped out listening to Charlie Parker, Oscar Peterson, Dizzy Gillespie, Coltrane, Monk, Sony Rollins, Bill Evans, Jimmy Giuffre. Mary would have to leave the room when he would groove in delirium of a Jim Morrison and Rimbaud to the limit again with Céline's, "To hell with reality, I want to die in music, not in reason or prose." There were only a few left in this country, who could dig it at the time. When it became too far out here, the French "put it in trust." Even Sachmo made fun of Bebop. Claude was lucky that he found me and Paul Bley in Cherry Valley who could groove with him as in our youth. He also invited the genius musicologist, collagist, filmmaker, Harry Smith to stay with them in Cooperstown and live in their studio as long as they could stand it, which was a good bit of time for them. Cooperstown also had a special kinship to the Frenchman . . . the rugged untamed nature in the work of James Fenimore Cooper.

Coincidentally, we were in San Francisco to see that changing city with its ever-changing scene usher in a new music to take the place of the old. It used to be a great jazz city. In the seventies, we would see Sonny Rollins play a small tourist trap club in North Beach for the cover charge of a two-drink minimum and play a few notes and leave. The big action was the go-go and disco joints. In the sixties we would see Janis Joplin and Big Brother at the Filmore and new psychedelic groups at the Avalon fill the house but when Bo Diddley came, only a handful knew him. He started his gig by saying, "And here I am now playing for you. Mercy, Mercy, Mercy." Glenn Todd and I would sit in an almost empty dive to hear Chet Baker who came out to begin a song and disappeared. So the Frenchman would act as a trustee, holding American music until new groups were created and the old would come back again. Certainly Bill Graham at the Filmore had seen the evolution before and came out of the great Harlem Latin tradition of the Palladium in NYC. But it was very sad for me to see Claude end up in a most unlikely place, a nursing home in backwoods Norwich, New York with a leg amputated begging me to get him some old jazz . . . "you know, some Bird." I bought him a little tape player and recorded some of his old LPs recalling his words, "Every day the DEAD idea kills real life, bubbles dominate actuality—they're emptying the trash cans of history." He was buried nearby and had a Catholic service. The same Catholicism that was his carnival, his bubble he delighted in busting. He also made fun of his religion and dressed up like a priest and nun in the tradition of artists, priests, poets do to expose all hypocrisies.

To understand his geography is immense in itself. When his friends Alain Jégou came to visit them during their waning days, Mary had fun counting all the places they had lived and came up with a total of

71. Mary had a favorite photo with Eisenhower digging her. She had been in an internment camp but still looked good. Her husband had parachuted behind enemy lines with no navigation and extra fuel tanks welded into the cargo planes and was found by the Bedouins. He helped lay the plans for the North African campaign that Ike said "was a crazy idea but it's all we got." Her first husband was an actor and dubber in Paris until he died of a heart attack. Claude was found on the streets of Paris by Pam Beach who brought him home. He spent the rest of his life with Mary Beach, whom he later married. They both worked every day at their writing, making collage and translating. At Lawrence Ferlinghetti's suggestion, they came to San Francisco the implication City Lights would publish his first novel, *Automatic Pilot*, but it was later published in mimeo format by Ed Sanders of Fuck You Press. Mary worked at City Lights with Ferlinghetti and established a lifelong friendship. While there, they translated Bob Kaufman and other Beats and were instrumental in getting him published by City Lights. They came to meet Allen Ginsberg at the Gough Street flat where Neal and Allen had just moved in to share it with me. I met Mary's daughter, Pam, during their tenure in San Francisco. They preferred to stay away from the "scene" and found out-of-the-way bars to drink and meet regular people from a variety of S.F. inhabitants. Claude liked to talk of his service in the French army in Algeria, so he and Mary found bars, during the time I knew them in San Francisco that were far away from any hippies, yippies or protesters, yet they agreed with the activity of protests and their friends' Ginsberg and Ferlinghetti's

political views. They made a lot of friends like the Portuguese bartender at one where Claude's antics included shitting on the floor over some kind of bet. He could get away with such antics like that and pissing in Norman Mailer's pocket when they lived in NYC.

They moved about carelessly taking all their work with them and losing a great deal of it when leaving a place. They had an apartment fire that ruined a lot of their work, but nevertheless they were very prolific. They worked with words and images every waking day of their lives. Pam tried to get them to purchase a house in Cooperstown with the front yard extending to the shore of Lake Otsego. A beautiful setting with only a two-block walk to the main street of a famous picturesque town. The house had been the Mohawk Indian Museum and was a fine structure. The only item between it and the lake was the statue of an Indian and his wolf. For some reason, they would only live in apartments, and spent Mary's inheritance packing up and moving and shipping all their paintings and belongings. At one point during the 80s with the emergence of money management scams, a money-manager cleaned them out of what they had left. From 1963 to 2006, they left Paris for San Francisco through the Panama Canal and arrived in San Francisco in 1963. They moved back to NYC on 9th & 3rd Ave. in 1965. Back to S.F. in 1966. Then Honolulu in 1967. Back to the Chelsea in 1969-70 and London for a while and then to Eastbourne for a few years. It was at that time *Kali Yug* was written as well as some books by Claude Pélieu-Washburn the new name for the English gentleman. He was Claude

Pélieu-Washburn living in England. "English twilight carries an old address around . . ." When in NYC and in England they visited with Burroughs a lot. Victor Bockris came to interview them and sent it back to us in Cherry Valley to publish in The Coldspring Journal. One line from Claude I remember was Claude telling Victor his (Victor's) time was shit! It was a very funny interview. Allen Ginsberg and Peter Orlovsky came to visit them during that time and Claude having fun with the story that he and Burroughs should walk on one side of the street so as not to be associated with Peter and Allen, who were in their farmer's drag (overalls) that they wore in Cherry Valley. In 1977 they moved to Mill Valley, CA; 1978 Cherry Valley and Cooperstown; 1979-83 to Jacksonville, Fl; 1983-84 back to Cooperstown in the apt. Harry Smith lived with them; 1992 Cherry Valley; 1993 back to Le Havre & Caen France; 1995 Albany and Cherry Valley; 1996 Norwich; 2002 Claude in nursing home; 2004 Mary lived alone in Cherry Valley.

Of course, Claude Pélieu was full of contradictions. He was lucky enough to find a benefactor in his life that enabled him to be of the leisure class, to be the artist he worked every day at becoming, but could never understand money, responsibilities and why other just didn't create in all their waking moments. Ironically too, he didn't understand the art scene in this country. How Nixon would increase the National Endowment to reward artists, "friends rewarding friends" became the phrase. It was through the outreach of such programs (at one time in the decade this book was written,) Carl Weissner called the government supported arts "subsidized lint." It was one of the arts organizations that lured him to Norwich, completely out of any cultural environment like he would have known in Paris or New York. Yes, they had small exhibits, but there was no one to attend. They won competitions at the Cooperstown Art Association and were exhibited next to what is called "Sunday painters" by those who had lived their lives in the artist bohemian tradition.

Meanwhile they were victimized by more scam artists, who took their work for shows hoping to give themselves credibility only to, in many cases, flee with their art. Such was the case in Norwich. In this respect he was naive, trusting and not fully aware of what to do with his own work after he created it. He and Mary left hundreds of their works scattered over the globe when they moved around. They both had early acclaim in France, which was legitimate, and a start, but fell victim to circumstance, if not geography in most cases afterwards. He didn't know how prophetic this book is. How the Seventies turned into the flamboyant disco era free from the intellectual/psychedelic "revolushun." The 80s music was also tired of the folksy protest hymns and the punks wanted to smash things up with heavy metal. That was right up Pélieu's alley. The Eighties were dominated by great cocaine wealth through all levels of society. The Blacks went to jail for snorting it and the Whites cleaned the money and had to build banks in Miami just as vaults for the cash. That money went into the banks of the Nineties yet into vaster schemes essentially Ponzi schemes with the country's wealth that had no assets, an economic virtual money derivatives of futures that had

18

no reality. All of the criminal enterprises and controls ended in his prophecy of yet another empire falling, its blood sucked dry.

Charles Plymell
January 2011

A WESTERN AT THE GATES OF HEAVEN

nature mumbles
the sky is fringed with golden red tonight

Highways bleed dawn-stones. Frost lisps all year long. Bare stones fill time. Your star-studded footsteps & flowers scream "no sooner written no sooner extinguished." An ink spot tells me that I'm not the toy of hazard.

KALI YUG EXPRESS, *COCA NEON CAMERA SUTRA*—grief banks are open day and night, laughter-banks too—waves carry bundles of tears away, and the *buskers* sleep in time's bed.

"When a finger points at the moon, the imbecile looks at the finger."

Good and bad news, via satellite, extraordinary, instantaneous news, sequences written above the landscapes, in smoke, on the deserted Technopolis sidewalks, in the echo chambers and the murmur in front of the reality studio, behind the TV jukeboxes, in the basement of the Videotheque of the Universe—crossing the oceans, the Great Plains, deserts, clambering down the mauve, snowy hills, wandering in arcades of slot-machines, from bar to bar—I see a neon sign, huge, great multicolored letters . . . "NO GOD NO PEACE . . . KNOW GOD KNOW PEACE . . . DAY-GLO FUN PACK" . . . wandering with the shadows, caught between two languages, wandering from hollow to hollow, escaping maturity, to the poem and prose kitchen, to routines, to the Brain Police, strolling on beaches seeing the old 50s and 60s gray film, the wall of lamentations of *Hollywoodstock Market* again, seeing again the huge hysterical and political circus in free fall . . . a super flash in the dew . . . I decided to write this book in any old way for just anyone. And for Charley Plymell and Joël Hubaut. *"My days have wandered away,"* blue in a wall of tea.

Crossbows, scents, miles of wind hanging onto a sex, jukeboxes and scatterings. Everything's damp, shining, wet, quivering, and the rain hides behind a curtain of aspen. A grieving seagull pukes a wisp of smoke, orange stomps, like these written words, films broadcast over every landscape, dying on the spongy, gray screen of everyday.

New York, Los Angeles, San Francisco, Dublin, London, Penzance, St. Ives, Beachy Head, Electric Rainbow Hill, Muddles Green, Coca Neon And Dreams For Sale. Softly grass-flesh cries out. Silence breaks into the flesh. I ignore academic and social grimaces. A shabby, purplish cloud deflates. Over there a lovely green grass coming from Kenya, cultivated on top of a mountain near a big blue lake—a floating typewriter over there.

Ink-solitude, gestures freed by patience & panic, the silence displaces a few drops of water, colors stolen from angels and children are reborn on a sprig of syringa.

Never slow down. Never. Hang onto light, like God. Then a wave of maple syrup. *"Get off my cloud Shitface!"*—you dig anecdotes, they say—in that case, my advice is to travel light. In the end all the nudes did go downstairs. Nostalgic ghosts return to the non-visions that dominate them, when unity exists in their deepest souls. They don't know how to waste time nor to get stoned, they don't know how to *take* the time, nor capture the wind. We're on earth, among the living, in the heart of the Electronic Democracy, in the Kingdom of the Flower-Age, and we know that Eternity is a big whirling thing. We don't need the meaning of a word explained to us.

I accost you in a shower of colors.
Those colors belong to the Planet.
We'll be neither worse nor better off.

It's by begging that we become writers, of course, ink lies, mikes jostle each other, reality overflows, energy versus logic—mud isn't against our having fun, demons sponsored that farce greatly— collective loneliness and absence of privacy may have awakened us, technology has given another meaning to life. Mist created man and woman, and those that want to alienate us at any price, they're not autonomous personalities . . . as for the rest? The *rest* weren't really inspired . . . the spinning of the Universe is very near to what we call madness, so, why did you lie down among the pigs with your history books? Start doing your thing.

A friend committed suicide in Cleveland . . . one morning waking up, he unhooked a gun and placed the cold, damp phallus in his mouth, then fired the trigger, and the bullet exploded in his mouth like a very powerful youngster . . . The Brain Police had already signed his death sentence. A prism-penis of hamburger-death dancing among flowers and trees, flashes modeling on the snarling, stupid mob's bloodshot eyes . . . (I heard of his death in Honolulu) . . . When you abandon cities you see all of reality—

silence and music translate your emotions word for word, image against image—our emotions have told us lately and invariably that the Universe is perfect, unwavering, & if I understand well, the governments of the Earth have really decided to save the Planet.

A twilight-boat capsizes with fairy tales.

A sharp pain breathes in the heart of England. *New Morning, American Beauty,* and Nashville's *Enamel*-gaze, the new sounds of Motor City fed by the wild winds of the Great Lakes—unsuspecting children go by while a dead leaf soars over them—they're told to hurry off to school, they shrug their shoulders . . . dolmens & menhir show off their beautiful white teeth, a silvery wave carries a teddy bear away.

COCA NEON

Coca Neon, grass vanishes behind the transistors of innocence.

Cities, mouth-taxis, blue zones, conscience-worlds, vaudeville, festivals, games, warm skies swallowed by lacerations, driftings, vanished throngs, Burger City, smells of pepper and mint, Mona Lisa ambushed in a neon-kaleidoscope toke . . . *Southern Pacific, Jefferson Airplane, the Fugs, The Twentieth Century Train, Cosmic Drag . . .* rebirth of neon, comix, *light shows*, automatic pilots, pebbles playing on the Heart-Strand, this world, yours, mine, ours—we were in the Valley of the Dead, everything was electrified, even the chirping of crickets—the planet's huge stammering on a *pinball machine* covered with blue fruit.

I think the cities are still there, Paris, Panama City, Honolulu, Mexcity, L.A., San Fran, Chicago, New York, London . . . Gasoline Alley, Magical Street, the Lower East Side, Haight, North Beach, Snow Hill, Muddles Green . . . Nothing has changed. The cities are still controlled by the Brain Police, cordoned off, dripping with neon . . . drugstores, videotheques, supermarkets, Polaroid Drag, pollution hole—the automatic pilot makes a tri-colored jump, falls back, exhausted, into the puke of a generation—but of course, he's a hero, shit! . . . it was a question of walking, waiting, spinning around, finding a good vein, surviving flat on the ground, back to the wall, gnawed by sickness and cramps, whirling with shadows, with corner-words of black cold and white hunger . . . That's what it was, police-cars, banal chumps, raids, identity controls, what happens in any megapolis. We watched the garlands of perforated veins, unreal titles . . . the old films rotted with the detritus of hunger, thirst, fear . . . the spoon, the eye-droppers, the shit heating slowly, & gray and red flowers returning from the clouds. You're either in or out of it—with a vague woman odor on a bench in a dive, very ordinary—with aging flesh, blade against blade. And you wake up in a gray dawn sick, you're always given a bad role. *Junkies* always tell the same story. There's nothing to understand, except what's told on movie posters . . . you pull out the nine of hearts from your sleeve, snow three of a kind! And blood beats in your temples . . . short-legged delirium, lisping identities toppling in the great belly-waters . . . sadness, Heart Break Passage, pop eyes, drifting away—black streets, nocturnal almonds, boiling lead dripping on congealed idling periods.

Nerves hesitate, plastered on the sex-gills, in the death-pit of oblivion. Un-translatable silences. We are on the right path, in blurs, inside, outside, and we live with our mouths closed at the end of the most beautiful night, a no-story wading outside of veins—a cabin in the sky—delta-lips dance on the wings of a missile, drunken gestures, semaphores of bone, aluminum and polyester trails . . . shrill whistles, flames, burned reeds, alfalfa fields set on fire, unkempt clouds all the way to your thighs, and the red mud of thousands of guys holding radars by hand.

Something turned white, swayed, flowed to the horizon, night, Obscure Vale, sorting out of stars, and at 13000 meters, in my sky, Navigator Flower . . . and sweet almond oil or carnation, protecting the grass in a dream's backseat . . . blazing screens, subtitle sounds, Immedia Video, rainy credits . . . and the slowness, among daylight's crockery, and the flesh that discovers itself automatically—so, how can you imagine anything? Intermission—that something that cracks like neon on Eternity's velvet index, attacking bare lips. Dead water. Rutting punches. Games of solitaire.

Expressways, penis gas-pumps, all in bloom . . . the massacre of chromosomes, so we had to make a break, inside, that is elsewhere, close-up, obeying the call of nerves—and to write all that in bulk, and to talk—writing it on water, sand and wind, on branches . . . giant billboards . . . 1963, November, the awful news, JFK is assassinated in Dallas—American troupes settle in Southeast Asia . . . *technicians* the CIA and KGB's dogs, napalmicans, *Air Opium Pentagon*, and then LBJ-HHH . . . fluid time tattooed with swells, leaks, the mad hitchhiking from North Beach to Monterey, Bodega Bay to Big Sur—a new consciousness was affirming itself, cracking the jukebox, like snapping teeth in grass wounded by frost. Arizona, New Mexico, sand mandalas take off, brown Mexican wisps agonize in the corn & black wheat fields, stones, turquoise curtains, wind choppers, and Indian flowers emptied of their sap. Mouth to mouth reanimated memory. Long flexible cocks making their way through blurs, in truth, the fiction-flux of something, and all the sounds of the world are more in tune, wider, more humane in spite of everything . . . like images opened with a knife in the Sierra, or in the flesh stores of Spanish Harlem . .

27

. ultramarine blue tearing at the Ocean Planet. And signs in the cutlery that night had nothing more to murmur. Empty shippers on the other side of the rink, flashes, communiqués, & from dawn to dusk swaying, with hands on hips.

Slowness. Ephemeral grimaces. We can only breathe in reality. And I wrote to William almost every day: *Agony to breathe here. Signed: The Frisco Kid . . .* then silence was transferred outside the ropes, the boxer was knotted up by a curt snapping of fingers, and on a stormy night's smooth brow a very soft word burst, that word could sleep at last, like a ping-pong ball . . . Realities? Those smiles so forced because of dreaming, living . . . the angel gets up, plays the electric organ, night overflows.

Frisco in the gangways of the eye. The crumbs of an old western. The one we were writing in Frisco, Tangier, New York, London, Mannheim—electronic fairies had something to do with it, and the Enchanters will come again, in a month, a year, with their bouquets of eyes and *fuck yous*, with Panama Rose, Rose Nebraska, Tim Leary *the Cosmic Whore, Xerox Punk,* Kali Yug, *Captain America and Snoopy . . .* I saw that day tattooed on a child's teeth—imagination's sparkling crime in the *Pranksters'* eyes, and the dead, as sad and grateful as gloves. There was no one in the Snow Subway.

Smiles, grimaces. With a spray can I wrote on the wall: THE SUN WILL SHINE WITHOUT YOU. And it was true. And it's still true. Then a cross on your sucker-eyes, a cross on the junkie, a cross on everything—daylight never ends, people mature on white metal, & the silence they impose on themselves isn't worth much—mechanics refuse to obey, electric fingers masturbate children who shit on the heads of their elders, they write on living rags, kill, loot, set fires, and the *Chorus Girls* are in the know . . . teargas fumes swallow mirrors and walls.

At that time, Allen, Peter & Gary were in India, Japan, Kerouac had left for Florida, Orlando or St. Petersburg, checking his satori-aim after having written *Big Sur*.

I drove day and night in blue silk. Dylan spiked light in Wichita, Kansas, cities were hungry and cold, the earth was warm as a child's spit. Sexual shards boiled by Lucy Mirror, dog-eye touching-mouth pebble, morphine within reach . . . the Angel takes off from Chinatown which was star-studded at the time . . . creased heavens, panes sticky with sperm, milk-revolver, emeralds stumble, blue grass blazes— the electronic music of Democracy, Virginia creeper drowned in Coca-Cola, a pink tornado, session *Hard Rock*, Dixie flutes, tubercular TV—strange to think of all that now, see how things have changed, people, the world, life . . . Nova Kim was with us, and Boo-Boo, wandering in British afternoons, with the latest *junkies*, sniffing fluid and silent anecdotes . . . and Sharky, with or without a mustache, was hiding in the gray voices of cops.

An empty suitcase abandoned in a hotel on Magical Street.

A melon colored moon explodes.

Desperate last words in a sticky dawn, CIA smells, odors of China in Cut City—primrose was my name, a tornado cut in naked eyes—*Image* Base, Nebraska-fugue, and *Blue Jack Ink* arranged eyes in time, with the Sepia Kid dying in Oaxaca like a simple sound.

And the others? Where are they? They're stomping somewhere.

Ten years, fifteen years already . . . everything happens . . . filmed echoes, morphine, hot bath, I'm raining, and the invisible stains of our generation explode—westerns and technologic counterpoints—a bathtub, an old hotel in Chinatown, a door open or shut . . . old sneers . . . North Beach, *City Lights,* a new world-consciousness, a painful *clash,* flipped out zazen . . . a robot can't recondition himself and flesh refuses to die in the dream's pocket.

News from *the Global Village* . . . Hippyland doesn't exist anymore. A dim-witted horde of imitators grasps what was written in heaven . . . like those guys who have never left the country of cheap red wine and checkered handkerchiefs . . . planetary hicks, Venusian boobs, and now those crazies shoot kids, think for you, and poison the grass that made eyes pop with wonder—we dive into the most distant universe with hallucinogens, our brain, and every day we draw a map of it, tripping in time and space, and the Life-Poem blooms, people come and go, and limitless powers of speech are carried off by rock 'n' roll, ZAPOKALYPSE!!!

Yoga Cut/up, conscience-brain, prosody and bopology, long trajectories. (And, tell me, do any of these things, neither here nor there, have anything to do with the banal stories of *drugs?* with crime? With the so-called discoveries of the *French Under- ground?*) . . . Hippyland doesn't exist anymore . . . the planet's going to blow up . . . Ku Klux Klan Kultur is seizing the Universe . . . and now *the sacrament of acid*—prisoners leave their

30

ghettos, the sun's blond guts are in a state of siege—
Hippyland doesn't exist anymore, Woodstock doesn't
exist either, Yippie's over, *diggers crazies and zippies*
have left, there's no one on the road, there are no roads
anymore, trees march spitting neon, electrified cloud
hold hands—how are they going to learn how to live
again? With their hearts, with their heads, under the sun,
in the wind, how? . . . void in a ball, a gold-fringed
scream in the blue fog, and shadows strip the days that
are now counted for us.

I have assembled these notes & tapes at *23
Poets' Street*, today baptized as *Gasoline Alley*. The
arrows of Sagittarius have created light, and shooting
stars beg for beautiful tresses.

Cigarette burns explode in empty places.

We were on the road, with millions of eyes,
insane dreams molded and rolled visions—the sky rid of
its fangs was proud of its freckles—a voice chewed on
angelica that the wind and frost had mistreated.

Arrows smeared with honey and *Majoun*. Arrows
shot by the rain passenger, at #23 Poets' Street, an
orange flower-girl who had a boy's ass—time has blown
up my colors, all sails set—time unsheathed that image,
this whispering odor-voice, I ENTERED, I LEFT . . . the
ice's broken, the mirror's empty, poets bleed on the
white keyboard of words—I is finally ME, I shuffled the
cards of conceit, and with my foot I reject those
thousands of hackneyed, filthy words lying in the dust of
Panama City, in the streets of London with the Tantric
wave-lengths of conscious- ness, moving from one end
of the earth to another.

Everything happens, all of a sudden things
happen, and Willy Lee's mad laughter falls back onto the

31

dream machine, it's written in the sky, old words explode at dawn, howling like wolves, a poem digs out vision—dwarfs limp on the screen, fink-computers think for you—we will never pay the tab that we owe the system. Everywhere robots beat, imprison, torture, kill, mutilate, repress, trafficking bodies and souls, brainwashing people. And millions of zombies chuckle, satisfied, overfed. They chuckle when young people leave the life they never wanted to change. Every day they win a cadaver and are upset if the sick commit the irreparable. Innocent windows inside shooting stars—we descend from water, wind, the sun and Earth, singing along with young light years, we're alive, we're breathing, we've recovered our health, we're free, and fairies dance, waves spout videocassettes setting the sky on fire, lets images speak.

'IN THE EARLY MORNING RAIN'

Ted Berrigan

Seven o'clock in the morning, silence's broken,
spatial music and the wind wound green wood.
Zigzags, broken stars, grab-bags, the mauve
haze on Beachy Head recalls things to me. The
Universe's a box of Danish Camembert—lights and
neons vacillate over parking lots, telling us that
wasted time keeps its secrets—a flame follows my
gaze, an instant has stolen the far north from the
chance-echo. Erased imprints, absences mistreated by
pain, dawns saturated by rain.
The smell of meat attacks the Universe.
Nothing can explain that cloud in the sky—
sequences and meditations—a music that cries laughs
and sends the world off to pee. A white pen scintillates
in the green grass, the Japanese cherry trees do
nothing but blossom, dew flows, bursts, swallows the
hills, and illuminates empty places.
The Musical Hyena has wrapped up Nixon's
rock in a pop-bag, the rest's thrown in the sinks along
with congealed spermatozoid. The others, tragically,
repeat themselves or imitate.
We've seen it all, we no longer want to
communicate in the center of that encirclement and with
the growing stupidity. The thief's wink isn't one of them,
the packaging-space is merely a scenic trick to restore
logic and morality of work. We should give nothing more
to beings or things.
The red dykes cried out:
"Stand up Hamlet! You faggot! The tide's rising!"
Like seagulls we must digest things together.

Screams—"Death! Death!", "Styles and Drag Queens!", "Proles of the world, caress each other!" "Bomb yourselves with excrement!" "Don't fight for the last crumbs!", "The Chinese invented trousers!"—in short, you dig their sort, good vibrations, *good karma,* nice style, a brotherly hand shake, a big smile in the way proles do . . . "anyone who has an orgasm's on the right," or "proles' assholes are always filthy", you know their sort, ugly, very ugly . . . then the poor guy makes fun of himself, *we* invoke the anxiety of the uprooted man, the crisis of civilization, the alienating silent majorities are caught in brawn, and my ass reflects all the colors of the rainbow. Zombies love their anti-personnel death-gadgets . . . after the psychedelic and electronic genocide . . . zombies and robots, sad suckers of goiters hanging between their legs, at the hour of socio-cultural braziers.

Sometimes, between two airports, everything's turned into music, the heavens erupt, the setting of shooting stars on fire as well as sexy messages, thanks to neon. The broadcasting of soft & flabby technologies in the videotheque of the Universe— *sex-fiction* and horrible convulsions—me, I'm dying of laughter and I'm very healthy, in spite of everything, therefore, I've won. I've returned with a few flipped out chromosomes.

ACTION—ASSAULT PHASE—we've cut our hair, our magnetic reading tables are covered with flowers. Not all stories end well, and people don't often dance in the streets. We're not always on the *sunny side* of the street. While waiting to see Malibu Beach & Hollywood again, we have to wander in space-time. Our audiotapes are the blueprints for survival for 1984. Operation *Capture & Multiply,* Operation *Wake Up*

People! The Dream is Over, operation *Ah! The Beautiful Classics! . . .* A Flip-Video under the stars, refrigerated jukeboxes, liquid air, heavy & slow water, and a neon-mirror . . . The bursting of poetic language and written, spoken, drawn and filmed advertisements . . . sweet hydrangeas and technology, flake-flowers on the windshield, bluish snow like sperm.

They killed what spun around void.

Avalanche-worlds, soft music, and dried sperm, crucified and an emaciated infinity . . . foamy stars wafting our sleepless nights, colliding with God, between the seen and the heard.

The tongue doesn't know what to think. Same with me. Ugliness straddles life. Making fun of oneself in the rain while figuring out the lines of the hand of someone else . . . Boredom furnishes the Universe's bunker secrets . . . Eyes, under ice, eat Swedish matches. A *sunbeam* fan-pubis containing the whole day . . . worn out snow, inserted vertigo into these blue landscapes, the wind curls and the flowers of the sea pulverize the poet's insane speech. The marsh-time- table eats from God's hand. A panorama was the carnivorous accomplice of time. My nerve's soul tells you to go to hell! . . .

35

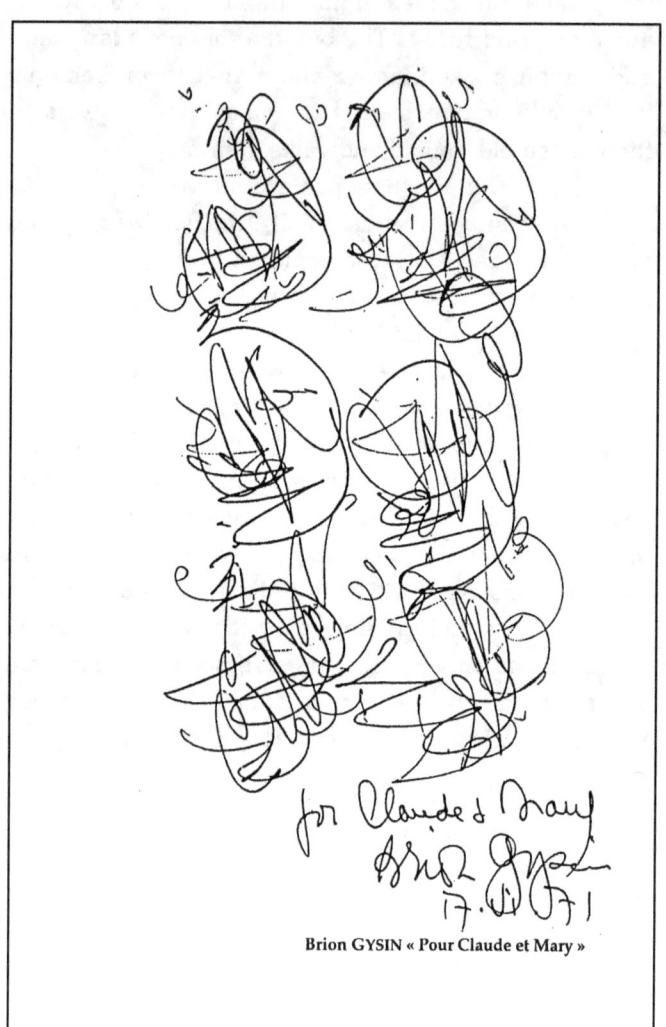

Brion GYSIN « Pour Claude et Mary »

CAN I DREAM AWAY THE SKY?

Sometimes rage dozes on a sheet of water. Death oozes out of your eye. A crooked laugh strokes the mirror—and there's nothing important that's worth mentioning, at least not now—I am free, therefore neutral, & you? . . . The road is ash-colored. The world's full of questions and answers, & after-dinner tricks. Don't apologize. And never explain yourself . . . Almond green on white silk . . . I'm   high . . . a spurt of silence—a flash of shade on the hills, and a few flakes of snow—the sky's on alert. Pollution has disfigured my landscapes, and you, lovely slaves, inhale it on these spaces bloated with stones . . . a bird perches on a branch, the greenness of the pine-grove fills the emptiness, a child's clear gaze casts away its parents' scowls. At the death of myths flowers survive. Small bites in the margins, little   cuts . . . Oh! The great cultural pregnancy! Hey! Here come the photographers! . . . the cloudy stream of wonderment, *DEATH ECHO FILES* . . . a cold, sour wind flattens the wild grasses that have survived. It was yesterday. . .

Whirlwinds. Myriads of elves and goblins. The earth thinks it's completely naked. So we must tell all and reject extreme misery . . . notes and smoke . . . images skip rope over the void. A perfectly human silence can serve language, but Spring brings back monsters that have barely left childhood. Immaturity is one of the reactions of expression.

Kapok guts, hamburgers mixed by electric hands, furtive gestures, bloody neon rots on the highway . . . children gathered cuttlefish, water-drop baubles, turbulent mandalas—the miracle's red core, and still more awareness, where nothing exists—I step aside, you're floundering . . . pure joy in the desert, an image of Big Sur, an image of Cherry Valley, hills covered with flowers, and the photographs develop howling.

The pale sun washes the city walls. Wind-battered stones squeak and recover their speech. I blow my own bubbles because one must scream in front of those doors. An old Christmas tree creaks in the shadow. Sleeping trees are no longer asleep—after silence, rain—it was yesterday . . . in a bottleneck of bumpers the Blue kid dreamed of tomorrow, perhaps . . . it was a Frisco rag mimeoed by cocaine crystals . . . since then I've had my share of fun. PARANOIA Warehouse is closed, like the Drugstore of the Sky—an enormous slice of blue dripping with grafts and screams, back-things uttered out loud, each silence possesses the world.

A white sound occupies the landscape and the night club of the Universe.

France in the world is like water in gas, *the country of no return,* TV-Mescaline, visions, planets, dawn bells, smokes, white whiskey, X-ray bullets, rock 'n' roll—I met Toscanini and St. Jerome (a very simple musical conversation)—mauve jukeboxes behind the hedge of dirty laundry, white roses caught with impassible, unmatchable rumors. The wind's got my tongue.

Indifference is the same all over. An immense collective isolation I won't complain about. Silence and music are busy. Nothing can annihilate my personal space. Water flows over comics with unreadable

38

poetry, pink pornography, with body and soul. We danced in the center of the mandala, on the toboggan of mad laughter. So, where are the elements of the announced answer?

I'm listening to Jimi Hendrix, a man and a guitar, a rainbow forever—a rainbow-man—Johnny Winter, Janis Joplin in the solar antechamber of Texas. . . the sun was coming to their mouths . . . Dead gods and Criminal Industries feed on carrion, fanfares stumble on blood-soaked fields. SATIVA, Heaven's Candy Store, Sidi Hidi dominates the throng, he contemplates wounded galaxies.

Smoke-filled heads and high seasons mumble, the *déjà vu* vanishes into thin air, the Universe's tears are forever linked to laughter's metal alloys— everything should be in flower, at high volume— pebbles snore and turn towards the light, the coffee is boiling hot, *Senior Service*, H, the windows are wide open, it's very cold, a pink sun . . . *DIG IT! DIG IT! DIG IT!*, without end . . . children's smiles make their way among gray, dirty words like burst tennis balls, real words, fat, stupid & filthy . . . Children are always dazzled, it's natural as they are innocent . . . then, suddenly, they die . . . cookbooks and newspapers close over them, they swallow a moral pill and land on the banks of adulthood. Like you and me. That's how we all became idiotic, absolutely! Regularly we watch childhood burn, and no one cares.

Fiction, fiction—the recent literary platitudes and the distribution of *wild* meat and beef bouillon have proved this for us—FICTION? The Tuberculosis Fairy handcuffs our inner eyes, and if I can believe the trace-instants that furnish our lives . . . now we must go, leave with the Universe's echoes . . . barely seen God hangs up, you made a collect call, Buddha is at the end of the line, he shuts up . . . Moloch Drosera, Kali Yug are listening. And we barely fill the planetary stage with our petty mental garbage.

HOT LEAD
IN THE HEDGE OF STARS

Horizons, arrows, flexible clouds, silent gestures describing the generation that was sitting on the electrified fence, clouds broken by the light breeze, electronic music flattening the wheat, screams poured into the Echo-Death dossier. The primroses and the forget-me-nots have disappeared. Must we tell you that nothing happens *just like that,* simply? Memories set on fire. Fairyland over Cielo Drive, Highway 1, Route 66, East Side & West Side Highways, New Jersey Turnpike, Spaghetti Junction, and further up SKYLAB, the *firmament,* and the wind that always chooses silence, like the dead flowers torn from the melodious soil. You can't survive with someone else's screams, you can't survive with the tics and yellow laughter of a generation, you can't survive with a single ideology or *ideas,* you can't survive with a panoply of words, images and sounds.

Back to speed, collage, cut/up, image after image, word for word, sound against sound, a cut/up in the anemic night wrapped in nylon, a poll of false news that fly from mouth to mouth, while silence with a damp cloth wipes away what's left of the 60s, that's to say *nothing.*

Sweet Jane water murmurs and carries comix away, flames follow eyes, and in the wind scattered doodles, in the heart of solitude that advances like an egg in the gray sky—on the back seat of a cloud an angel strums an electric guitar—the wild music germinates around an endless morning.

41

Horses gallop in alfalfa fields. Blue and green hills hurtle down a silvery trail with white clouds under a black sky. And on the shelf of oblivion *Speedway Road*, dimly in the rain. The landscape makes its bed in a whirlwind of whispers—under a thin layer of clouds the star studded polygon in the vein tree—solitude smokes in the darkness, lilacs lose themselves. A mint leaf tells me that I'm still alive.

THE

SILENCE

CRACKS

A

DANCER

PLACES

A

KISS

ON

THE

JUKEBOX

Electric Rainbow Hill, 5 am, the purple fog. 5 am, great cold in fire's deserted bed. The gold of the rising sun sinks into the pine forest. The frozen pond will be incapable of predicting the future.

The future? *Is Today Tomorrow?* Ray Johnson wrote this to Ruth Szowie: *I wore my pink wig today?* The future? *Poetry should be sold like Coca-Cola*—the boiling tea steams up the night's shelter—the purple fog fills my heart. Sinister information, horrible events, light ravages the dying night. Raw winter's silent spasms, grass flakes on the window panes.

Colors stream, the white cliffs close the march—frost bombards dawn—a parade of trucks shimmer on the highway. Sounds stifled into sandwiches and a few flames straddle the blue spray.

Vitamin C pills address Sweet Williams familiarly. Ann's here to pick flowers (between two planes) without giving them names.

SKYLAB is saved, the astronauts have returned after 28 days, a spectacular rescue. And during that time the Nixons struggled in the nuclear cramp basin. We chase butterflies, we pick roses, we're happy in this basket of hair, June's breezes chew on reality.

Rumors. Vacationed carcasses. Released skeletons. A marmalade of bodies. Allen will be here next week.

Doctor Leary says that the Universe's perfect, and I think the world's sordid, to high heaven . . . we live with or without masks, on the fringe of institutions, and we sometimes speak beside nature, near reality—but, nevertheless we speak a 'social language' in the heart of explosions of violence, dominated by our own *media*, by our own myths, we speak *our* time, laminated by the most repressive structures. We're suffocating. It's 'this & that' say some—let's send them back to back into the old suffocating film—the control machine has become more and more discrete and efficient.

"I'm going to get a tan on your tombs", murmured James Bond to Dick Tracy and Modesty Blaise, while Tito Vulvo masturbates in the bourgeois columns of *The Social Vice.*

Our dynamic structures, laden with eternal
and alienating values that obsess the sexual
proletariat.

Neuron panic.

THE COMPUTER LOST IN THE ELECTRONIC HEART
OF AN ENGLISH TIBET

Anguish reinforces the consumer's vanity which is chemically poisoned.

Evil gadgets, flashes, technological conjuring tricks, etc. Time-eaters come from the School-that-Stinks, and tirelessly repeats the Space Opera, sponsored by a brand of soap. We're on the fringe of profound debility and we're in space. We're committed to nothing, and nothing disengages us. We're the accelerations of conflict. We get all the messages. We are the *MESS-AGE*—cattle doze in mud, total spectacle—'The Flipped Out In The Middle Of Nowhere', who will smash our last illusions?

Corny meditations, manipulations, provocations, etc. Robots are using their heads. Flesh cracks. The teeth of our minds are chattering. The rest collapses. It ain't by chance if the infirm are agitated. It ain't by chance that there are so many sick violent people. We're entering the Era of Disappearance. And for those who have atomized their brains there isn't much left of their cerebral crust not even an Electronic Tibet, all that's left is a message of flickering pain in the gray film of the daily grind. Memory recall tells us that there is only one life, that there is only one world.

A voice in tears, and beyond the reality of freckles calibrated by Springtime tell us that the Brain Police have no visions.

A spectacle-landscape in the herbarium is in my heart, the bestiary in my head. Supernatural pink silhouettes and the sounds of water—how to describe

the white hot rings that sleep in the river's bed?—
Words mustn't complicate the lives of images.

Robots' syntax is frozen in heavy metal.
Mulberry trees hate thistles. Hills invaded by gorse, by
blue-bell lamps, by moon flowers—the thousand
wonders of fair weather, voluptuous waves, and the
songs sinking into our solitude.

I can't seem to answer such questions.

A claw against the livid sky. An ageless fog.
Someone is going to pull his hair out again. Who
wants to have his head on his shoulders? We're rich in
laughter, we should be rich in everything, even dollars.

A collision of all the suns—good and bad
news—A secret fire, in my image, the Universe is
partying, and there are still people who, *with weapons
in their hands, etc, etc.,*—those fluorescent morons
haven't yet understood that life gets its source in the
bare lips of space. They're not the only ones.

The episode *Vietnam Parking Lot Blues* is over,
erased. The snows have melted and wander around
alone. Fair weather will persist.

We breathe in the center of electric mosaics. The
film will be unpleasant, at times, frightening, unbearable.

Forget-me-not telegrams in the hobo's pocket,
realities stripped by ashes and hazes—pearls
flow, drip, explode and mix with butterfly wings—
everything lives and relives intently, like the sexy
telegrams in the wind's pocket.

VIA SATELLITE

A star dives into the sky's fur—who dares to write on my back?—The wrong side of a word? The skin of a sob?

What is there to say? (Your applause is taped by death TV, *The Big Cosmic Pancake)*. Yesterday, on the beach, a loud scream, followed by a black flame, announced that night will not submit to neon.

Neon beheading the shadow's spire—time's traces die on the screen—THE SKY'S HOWL.

And just at the corner of night, trees in flames shed their skin, colors breathe, the moon rips the boisterous silk of a pale sky—we start to drink and smoke, we fall asleep beaming, we awaken sick—ultraviolet in flesh and bones drags neon onto the beach. Rainbows meet just on the corner of night. Shadow and light mosaics.

The landscape makes its bed in the watershed of reality. Music. Savage embraces. Shipwrecks. Clouds are unaware of rumors and clamors, good and bad news, the clouds put to sea. Pine cones explode in the fire, laughter crackles in the chimney.

Day is breaking, turbulent. A world glitters in the cry of a seagull, every subject is rolled by slow waters.

Poetry, worlds and erasures, and on the arm of the sun, in one fell swoop, dawn's golden mouth.

Instant, reality, comix, Polaroid scenery.

In front of my TVs I open my eyes on what I've forgotten since 1970. We're on the tracks of the Villains of Space. We dream between our walls. We know that there are billions of galaxies in the Universe, and that all the living mechanisms, from the infinitely small to the infinitely large, pass from inanimate to animate. We know that God is the witness to that will. Men created Heaven and Earth.

What are our technical skills?

We are feeble astronomers, and what is left of our good sense remains in suspense, near a planet I used to call NOT TO BE DOUBTED.

Poets are all like their fellow creatures, consumers, dominated by the Brain Police and Sexual Bureaucracy.

Pollution and overpopulation will be stuck in the nuclear cramp basins. For a long time, the password was: NERVOUS DEPRESSION FOREVER. We should be wary of that defect, of disease, of old artistic concepts, of feelings of equality, and properly fix the operation: *IT'S ALWAYS SUNDAY.*

Polaroid hamburgers over cucumber-cities.

The integral transformation of citizens above suspicion. A pre-selection of ordinary and simple-minded people on the electronic keyboard. The electronic memory of all the televised deaths. Operation *FOR MEN WHO ARE MEN*—a light touch on social troubles and the psychodramas that ravage the Western paranoid nations—troubles unmaliciously caused by the retarded who haven't entered the twentieth century emotionally. Operation *LET US FINISH OUR DAYS AT EASE.*

Equality feelings, the end of prejudice, the abolition of money, *fans & pop stars* smoke brawn, operation *SWEET MAMA*—we hold our loved ones dear, don't we?—We have nerves of steel and the pills that help, our personal objects and instantaneous memories only survive by electronic impulse. Our power (I cannot find another word) doesn't depend on a minority. Operation *SEX DISPLAYED.* Under the Florida sky, operation *WE'VE GOT CHUTZPAH,* and nothing underneath, except for an old sprawling city, unaware of love and hate. A stencil-city saturated with neon, skyscrapers and purple fog. The electronic news on *Watermelon Street* disappears behind the blond mists that rise from the black streets and along the *skyway* the headlights of a million cars twinkle. On the side I think that those robots were maybe happy teenagers, high and unthinking. Maybe. Maybe not. It doesn't matter.

KwammMM! KAPOW! Zonk! Ouch! Zzzziing!

Habit? A murmur? A napkin? A finger-bowl? A pink flesh taxi?

Freak & Funky, inky-dinky parlez-vous . . . In the purple fog of Metropolis, or in the blue fog of Gun Hill, the last electrified minutes explode one after another . . . it was yesterday (but what does today mean?), nothing, I guess, absolutely nothing— the global village changes at the speed of light—we're here, we're elsewhere, we're there, we're not there, we keep silent together.

They talk about Nixon's genetic characteristics, Kissinger-*Folamour* & Mao's chromosome anomalies as well as speed freak Hitler's as well as the Pentagon and the Kremlin monsters who all came into the world with a pair of abnormal chromosomes. (Like the Villains of Space, like loathsome Beings. And there are many of them. I will introduce you to a few.

49

The Masked Cucumber, the Venusian Banana, Stinking-Cloud, the Ravaged Nippon, Red Charlotte, the Mad Anti-Semite, the Recycled Wog, Zorba the Schmuck, Hamburger Fart, the Catatonic Hippy, Jew Fart, Jose Bravo, Chopstick Charlie, the Masked lobster, Shit-On-A-Stick, the one-legged Negro, Tinker-toy Papa, the Dumb Structuralism, the Venerable Prick, the poxed Truffle, Johnny Guitar, the Talented Aborigine, the Sophisticated Prole, the Spatial Drawer, the Blue Monkey, the Musical Sleeping-Bag, James Bond, Modesty Blaise, Flesh Gordon, Henry Slap, Lady Punk Queen, the SS in Skirts, the Flying Mama, the Committed Waitress, the Introverted Terrorist, the Shitty Galaxy, the Cosmic Hooker, the Asthmatic Panther, Absolute Gratitude or the Courageous Publisher, the Conclusion Card Shark, *Modes Et Travelos,* and many others who have crossed the border of ugliness and filled your ashtrays.

Operation *CASH FOR TRASH.*

TIP OFF THE 'CREEP'
OR EAT MY LUNCH CAPTAIN AMERICA
SO WHO OWNS DEATH TV?

Richard Nixon's cronies are not the heroes of the American conscience. Seen from afar or near those incidents must not recur too often. That's the opinion of the DICK TRACY TV *brain trust.*

With the erosion of the dollar, the great counter-revolutionary peace and the Watergate affair, soybean flies away. Bad business for the US that assures 90% of it on the worldwide market. Since then the environmental politics have changed, and only the leftist side of the public believes in the good intentions of one or the other. Watergate?—a tragedy for Richard Milhouse Nixon—a catastrophe for the Industrial Military complex. Nixonoids and napalmicans debunked by Congress and the Senate. The future for the republicans is erased for several decades. But is that *really* a tragedy?

Could it be a scenario imagined by the Villains of Space?

Could it be a bit of science (political) fiction?

Could it be a conspiracy at the service of demoniacal forces of the control powers, of sex and blood?

Could it be the terrorist universe that inspired Televised Death?

Watergate? Could it be a puberty-reaction of Margaret Mitchell's?

Could it be . . .

By God! Kill those Commies! Smash these gooks! Knock out the fags! Fuck the goddamn Blacks!"... We're on the edge of the precipice.

How can we depopulate the planet?

Can we intervene where the real dangers are shown?

Can we take sides?

Nixon and Brezhnev measure the power of flux and reflux.

A new world. A new peace. A risk to run—a great risk if we dance—businessmen plugged into the dwarfs of space no longer have any visiting cards. You will see them in Palm Beach, on the Champs Élysées and Sunset Strip. You can meet them at Joe Banana's, at Max's Kansas City, on Madison Avenue and Withoutjoy Street, you may meet them in the corridors of the Pentagon and the Snow Subway, bump into them here and there, talk to them, touch them, and you'll notice that they will reveal their scornful audacity.

Operation "LISTEN TO EACH OTHER I AM THE STATE", or "THE GOSPEL ACCORDING TO YOUR NEIGHBORS" . . . meanwhile the SKYLAB guys photograph fields of stars, they are expected back tomorrow, Friday afternoon . . . I think that all this is logical and admirable.

Don't hang up if you have no collective importance. If you are merely an *individual* it's not good form to be listened to.

Watch out!—the Brain Police have read THE GRAY AND INVISIBLE GENERATION—operation "MINIMIZE AND SUBDIVIDE . . . "The agents and dealers of the CIA have also read *the invisible generation* by inspector Lee of the Nova Police . . . spy cameras in the video library of the Universe work well. Doctor Leary was the first victim of the MITCHELL- HALDEMAN-DEAN-McCORD-LIDDY & Co. computer . . . we'll find them again in the JUKEBOX-TV special edition that has no economic future . . . thus Nixon takes an additional dimension.

Secret agents, unemployed spies, psychopaths, policemen and agitators prevent the events from being known.

Electronic cameras create a psychological shock that disconcert the voters, ordinary citizens and feeble militants, those cameras erase the sexy message.

STATION ORANGE doesn't answer anymore.

Super Kool doesn't have a particular position to defend. Neither does Doctor Strangelove. Sergeant Pepper has taken the Chinese in charge. Captain America is frightened by the cost of operation "WHITE TRASH", thought up by the members of CREEP. John Dean has promised to tell all next week.

The growth of police power on our planet won't be interrupted by a new orientation of the US, USSR and Red China, even less by a revolution . . . there will be no revolution . . . thinkers and researchers that manipulate nations and masses are liberal, the sexual proletariat, the middle classes and the silent majorities are totalitarian . . . a few photos, a flash on the screen, turn the page, come in, leave . . . in eleven years 1984 . . . a new mythology . . . Apocalypse . . . John Wayne is surely one of them. And if we don't watch out we will (consciously or unconsciously) be obliged to obey their suggestions. Children born that day, "the

Watergate Generation", will soon be victims of accidents on the road, legal overdoses and political attacks.

"Hail to anarchy!" cried Senator Cheap. The effect was slimy.

The new way of seeing and hearing has the floor. Now listen to what the Blockade Planet has to say.

The "TRAUMA" team (dissident faction of *"Modes Et Travelos"*) has infiltrated the sewers of the White House. Jet of infrasonic sperm in the Washington sky. (Dick Gregory writes to Nixon, congratulating him for not having a single Black man in his German Administration.) The President and Perry Mason are going to examine the bilateral problems with lasers.

And no flowers for the shit-eating Chinks, Kissinger . . . you haven't understood Henry, is that clear?"

"Jawohl, Herr Nixon! Very clear, chief!"

Henry Tinkerer is a flexible person, intelligent, tricky, alert. It's undeniable. . . .

"Too bad that Bob Dylan and Golda aren't in on it", murmured the Medieval Groupie to Modesty Blaise who was distractedly masturbating a catatonic hippie.

"How can we get Doctor Leary out of that shithole?"

"Uh . . . you know, uh . . . the tab will be sizable . . ."

Operation "FLAMBOYANT DEATH"—Nixon and Brezhnev at Camp David, with a few hundred fags in uniform and thousands of call girls in heat—Operation "Salt Peanuts" . . . Nixon is learning

54

how to use a samovar, after having licked Mao's twat with chopsticks, nothing could be easier . . . Brezhnev is impressed, he distributes false passports to all the Jews he bumps into in Disneyland, and Chopstick Charlie becomes a pollster . . . Pat Nixon smeared with vaginal salve is transferred from one body to the next regardless of American traditions.

Livid Europe (between the pear and the cheese) pursues the hallucinating operation "LETS FLOAT ALONG TOGETHER".

Since she has been shut in John Mitchell's gelatin, Martha Muffburger has become schizophrenic. Who wouldn't be if we take into account what she has been forced to endure. John, Rat-Prick was his false name when he gave the green light to the CREEP conspirators.

The US assures 90% of the views on the science of blood.

Is it some kind of reaction?

"Kill those lousy Commies!" . . . they're known, classified, registered . . . a new world of businessmen in the halls of scorn.

They will, of course be obliged to die.

NEIGHBORS?

IMPERIAL POLICE . . . Fiction-Police . . . supplementary dimension of the Nova Police SUB-DIVIDED by electronic cameras.

ORANGE ANSWERS STATION STRANGE-LOVE.

TRASH frightened people a long time ago.

Totalitarian development.

Will surely be obliged to die, like most of the poor children. We're on the same page.

55

"Viva TRAUMA!" . . . a new way of being in the sky . . . "and no flowers! Is that clear?" . . . jack-off tab and fictitious name impressing the hallucinating left winger. Soy and dollars fly away . . . the villains of space and the nixonoids haven't changed . . . Could it be? . . . Sex and Power? . . . a great risk in dancing—devilish visiting cards—Televised Death reveals its unimportant audaciousness in the middle of those fields of stars. INSPECTOR UNIVERSE'S GOSPEL . . . From now on Lee will sort out events and sexy messages.

STATION WHITE is to be defended, that's obvious. Promises to tell all. New orientation. The proleratprick was in on it?

1984 . . . on our guard.

Road accidents.

White-House overdoses.

Legal attacks.

Chinese smiles between the shoulders.

Planet-Blockade has the floor.

Bilateral jets of sperm have you understood me? "Too bad that Bob and Blaise weren't at Camp David" . . . "and Leary?" . . . SALT PEANUTS . . . Nix-Mao from one body to the other, livid, swallowing my breakfast with chopsticks. An environmental matter, catastrophe, scenario imagined by the force of death. Mitchell started it all. The Americans watch. We're on the edge of perhaps...

Brezhnev, a great risk.

One and the other, gray, invisible. They photograph you as you speak.

"So, what about the future for the gray and invisible generation?"

"Rat-Prick won't change the face of the world."
Agitators won't erase my particular position.

Operation "CREEP", John Dean interrupts me through my pages, we will parachute him into the W. C. Fields Museum . . . in eleven years John Wayne will have expired, a victim of his own slimy effects.

Now, listen to the White House.

We're going to examine Kissinger's shit. Henry Tinkerer is a flamboyant groupie, "Fashion and Call Girls" . . . it was a matter of kidnaping extremist leaders and to sequester the clowns of the Democratic Convention "SUCK MIAMI'S TWAT". Martha, Pat, John and "The Screaming Faggot" on the world market.

TIP OFF THE CREEP AND DON'T BUG ME, HONEY. . . Milhouse Nixon in the heart of the tragedy. A terrorist universe where silence is essential.

"Smash those gooks! Kill that dirty Black! Twice! Thrice! He's the one, by God! And he squeals a lot!"

How to depopulate that slimy zone?

A new peace imagined and programmed by the Pentagon runts. They can be heard plugged into the British asshole, operation "DON'T HANG UP, DON'T SHAKE THE COCONUT TREE!" . . . could anyone take sides?

CIA brain read the other edition.

Hidden camera for the cops.

Super Kool was tough. The cost of the operation? A revolution . . . a few photos and you obey their suggestions.

The Senator fine-combs the CREEP members into the sewers of Washington. The Chink eaters of bosses have disguised themselves into catatonic faggots, nuts up to their ears, chewing on little balls of Vietnamese opium. Chopstick Charlie imprisoned since the beginning by the conspirators who put sneezing powder in Nixon's samovar.

US soybean-erosion, 90% of the sexual affair on the world market. And in full view the Nixonoids make a forced landing on Archibald Cox's table.

GOD BLESS AMERICA . . . even John Wayne who's in the sewers of heaven.

Big Jake, The Duke, an orange shock on the page.

Is it a mistake?

A political-fiction affair?

Blood here and there, is it Pentagon-audacity?

"LISTEN TO YOUR LUCKY STARS . . ."

"DON'T ADMIT A THING EVER . . ."

Televised Death in the special edition of SUPER KOOL.

EAT MY LUNCH, TIP OFF THE BRAIN POLICE, LISTEN TO YOUR NEIGHBORS.

A great risk in running. The computer always retains the sexy message. The global village disappears in the green fog ventilated by New York. Sally Harmony vanishes, carried away by a jet of infrasonic sperm.

A NEON ROSE-WINDOW
DIES ON THE HORIZON

Your brain has been eroded by realities, you took your time, and it was all pretty horrible. Some people blubber, because of their hatreds. Small bites, small cuts . . . When myths die flowers survive. No more bets. Others weave their multicolored deaths, shake hands, talk and chatter. They have neither enemies nor friends. They say it's a sign of despair.

Silvery slaps punctuate the course of history with cloudy streams of eternity.

Regrettable incidents, explosions in Belfast . . . Dublin recalls its ambassador . . . the codfish war . . . demonstrators brandish pickets, "IRA = Waffen SS", "Down with the Irish revolution!"—Representatives from African States are molested by drugged *skinheads*, ether and benzedrine, yells, "Bugger off Brilloheads! Wogs out! Get stuffed Niggers!" . . . here and there such incidents cause stirs—young people in sport cars in front of Salvation Army canteens mocking the faces of the jobless, the Chinese fiddle about the heavy gates of their commercial missions.

An old paralytic woman in her wheel-chair, waves a banner . . . "Jesus Christ is against drugs! Stop pornography! God Save The Queen!" . . . A trip all the way to the end of mediocrity in the streets of the world.

Programmers demonstrate against striking miners. "You see, those assholes are incapable of doing anything else, and then proles are born to work" . . . "It's always the same story when people don't know how to be content with what they have" . . .

A half-wit starts on a Marxist analysis of the audio-visual empire, slowly dossiers and files come to the surface with Echo-Death archives.

Chained onto the street lamps of Lord North Street obese militants start a hunger strike.

The red dykes and the fluorescent queers mix with the blue sounds of television sets that are never weary of dying.

Intox, Intox, INTOX. (A kid is reading a story about drugs in a widely circulated weekly magazine. And then he swallows a little too much codeine, sniffs glue, and gets high on cough syrup. His myths only hold up because of a venomous article. He'll be poisoned for life, but he might succeed to pierce the grayish screen of time's tune, sing its songs) . . . the dead have no stories to tell. God isn't in the know.

"The time goes by. You can't see time go by", a lady, who knows what she's talking about, told me.

It was yesterday. A long jerky film, lush with hundreds of magnetic tapes . . . where are the heroes? What has become of them? Are they dead? Are they alive? Stuffed? . . . it was yesterday . . . they have grown old, simply. They have become doddery and are now in lab-museums, on campuses, some of them had succeeded in *showbiz* and politics, others returned to their parents' bar, or grocery store or garage. The two poles of the future have taken them in charge. They didn't even have time to wave an eventual white flag.

All the world's follies are in your eyes. Sometimes it even comes to pass that we are happy and rich. Almost all writers have made themselves understood—signals twinkle in the sky—men and women twist in pain before the cold eyes of the cameras. The kind of pain we show, always, in any place, in short, we don't think, we pray, we advance, we recoil, we light up inwardly, we try to be happy, free, no nuances, then tragedies happen, we chat, as we drink alcohol, we laugh, we cry, and God calls the police . . . *there are strangers in my house* . . . they came yesterday, they must go to Nepal, they're here, they *occupy everything*.

They surface. It was yesterday. A mark on history. Sometimes we happen to understand. Intox. Intox, INTOX. Empire-sounds in the archives of coughs—"time goes round" it speaks—myths die on the grayish screen, *les jeux sont faits* . . . they're here, they *occupy* . . . and, of course they evoke brotherhood and good vibrations, they bore you stiff. They take over your personal space. A wave of bouillon and macrobiotic grub slips onto the lawn, a hurricane of greasy papers and used Tampax, the strings of an old guitar squeak and scratch the silence. It was yesterday . . . two shells of buckshot in the blue sky . . . I really don't care.

"Suck me but don't put it in me!" . . . a guy in black leather has repeated that for the last six months, desperately, he tries to resemble Jim Morrison. Will he fall apart, yes or no? . . . in short, he goes to Switzerland to make his tapes, then events come to pass, a parenthesis of gestures and facts, enigmas, variable distances and lateness between the seen and the heard . . . The regulars at Bilgray's Tropico come and go in the sky, shivering in their shrouds.

Ironworks and vacant lots.

The windows of the *American Express office* are shattered.

Cops on horseback charge the demonstrators.

GIs on furlough distribute tracts. A procession of Scottish communists chant orders (they are on the side of those demanding potato peels.) All that is very original, a fiesta in the streets . . . "Suck me but don't put it in!" . . . a few militants demonstrate, a vague story of washing-machines and community Tampax.

Sun in shining on Hyde Park.

Guitars are plugged into bottles of butane gas.

Processions, Pepsi-Cola, bouillon, hot-dogs.

Perched on wooden crate a priest babbles into a loud-speaker.

Ragged underwear floats over the roofs.

Nuns lift their skirts to piss on the flowers placed at the foot of the war memorial.

A gang-bang of businessmen at the *Piccadilly Hotel*. In filthy buildings in Notting Hill junkies inject light.

"Suck me but don't put it in!"—Subway exits puke thousands of commuters—Trafalgar Square is ravaged by vaginal salve, pigeons agonize in the slime. Dense traffic. Pedestrians jostled each other. Pubs and movie houses are open, cabarets and *sex-shops* too. A huge portrait of Bogart fills the facade of a building. French tourists bray and do their business through their mouths . . . people come to shop at *The Fashion Beads & Jeans,* high-heeled Italian boots reimbursed by Social Security, blue jeans made in Belgium . . . a catatonic Hippie yells, he drank too many Pink Ladies, he's flipped out, bad vibes . . . "Where are the photographers!" "Where are the photographers!"—he vanishes swallowed by the flashes from a pinball machine—the moon rises in a sky paved with neon lights. Japanese tourists harnessed with gadgets and gimmicks go by noiselessly.—The Jap Generation! Banzai Buddhahead! . . . neon like heavy makeup lights up faces that look like those of wax dolls. I drank a whole bottle of gin. I feel good. I advance. I don't touch the ground. I walk towards Saint James= on an empty tin can, I race along, piloting dangerously. I land in a street where there are nothing but Chinese restaurants, the worst in the world except for those in Paris, if I remember correctly . . . "Get back gooks! Get back dirty midgets! Tora! Tora!" . . . no one pays attention to me. I crash into a bunch of garbage cans. Three fetuses roll into the gutter. I upset a bunch of crates full of rotten, spongy vegetables. "Suck me but don't put it in!", I sing at the top of my voice . . . a band of *skinheads* . . . they're fixing the preps of a Pakistani with the lid of a tin can, some are waving shards of glass. I spit three times to hex them. I penetrate night's flesh, going through a jade screen I bump into violence . . . specters are copulating in hammocks . . . dead flowers hang from the windows of a private mansion. (Good God! That's where I was to meet the cultural attaché, I hope there's an elevator.)

RUSTIC SCENE IN SUSSEX

There are cadavers that jack off, virus-beings that want to relive in your body, they want to train your soul.

Sitting on a case of munitions a Scottish parachutist tries to milk the Holy Virgin. Catholic priest place bombs in movie houses. Riots, atrocities, repression—Protestants cast Catholics into huge ovens, young men attack military convoys, an endless day of violence begins.

Here, people drink, converse and laugh together, others dream. In the streets children are beaten by the police, the wounded are machine-gunned on the ground. A haze of anguish and fear envelops the squared-off town. Inconsolable the children fall asleep . . . the presence of the killers reassures those who swallow their words, bad magic—I went through all that, shocked, but indifferent—Later on I found myself at Lord Shmuck's house, there were a few famous names there . . .

"Please go into the living-room for coffee and liqueurs!"

"With pleasure . . . may I consult your collection of old manuscripts?"

"Of course, my dear, of course, I'm delighted, make yourself at home . . ."

An old member of the secret services make a great effect telling abominable stories. (That man is sick, I said to myself) sick, maybe even dangerous . . . A plump lady wiggles and talks about the *Beatniks, Hippies,* she's the wife of a BP man . . . Sir Euh-Euh is also there and Lord Whosamajig, a good old sausage with a veiny face, a fat farmer from the region is there too, a bunch of more or less ugly women, all of them very stupid. I wasn't at all surprise by it all. I'm used to it. In small doses it's even amusing. And very normal. As a matter of fact I have a lot of fun.

A little drunk and high I profit by it to become very boorish, impertinent. Not a single dwarf will attack me physically.

A historian, through a lackey carrying a note on a silver tray engraved at the Sussex crappers, the note saying that I'm indecent. Governesses and *babysitters* take the annoying ugly, stupid brats away who were giggling on couches and hissing behind heavy drapes.

"You old sluts! Slaves! Don't alienate those dear little shits!" I said out loud.

A thirty-five year old Immigration officer was there, with long hair, of course, face ravaged by vestiges of acne. A young blonde girl apparently in love, pierces the little violet pimp where little pearls of pus shine.

Those aphasic calves and huge cows are as ugly and stupid as their servants.

The chauffeurs are all in the kitchens.

And to think that tomorrow at noon we'll see all those monsters alive.

I swallow two pills of Benzedrine. Personally I'm having a lot of fun. It feels like being in an old 50s film, residues of Greenwich Villages, ex-beatniks . . . only missing Perry Mason and Flash Gordon, and the token Black. There must be one somewhere. May he's in the garden, jacking off furiously? . . . I say: "Where are the Blacks of yesteryear??" . . . Some youngsters are rolling cigarettes, and passers-by smile indulgently, except for an avant-garde French poet, a guy who knows who isn't taken in . . . he's always afraid that some Hippie in civilian clothes will drop drugs in his lemonade . . . he's an ex-Lettriste very much in favor . . . one time, his wife panicked and threw an ounce of hash in the garbage, to protect her dear little ones . . . One of their guests had mistaken a bar of Pakistani hash for chocolate, his sight was getting bad as of a long time ago. He ate the bar in secret, that fool! . . . two ounces in one day! . . . expensive, hard to take! . . . in short, a half hour later the guy smiles for the first time in forty years, as high as a kite, wanting to hear some real rock, dancing with the broads, and he started to insult his wife and son, who at nineteen knew where his responsibilities were and about the things that are done and not done.

"Well, you see, one must invest carefully, we financiers don't feel responsible . . ."

Well, my dear, I'm talking to you and I'm not afraid to say that I'm anti-Semitic!"

A member of Parliament was making a speech about the Common Market.

Satisfied grins from one and the other.

I thought it very amusing, at least more fun than the *hip* parties where they dedicate books and pamphlets and poetry chapbooks, where all the good vibes are unpacked, and where you have to sit in a circle around the chief guru and listen to the last LP sung by the fool—Oh but, here comes the Swami, the spiritual cop with the gray teeth, Ass Boom Ramdam, the so-called Breath, alias Ali the Puffer, an expert in breathing, bending in half with a coughing fit since he left his Brooklyn cave—scared and frigid beast talked about the Reich . . . a Maoist crouched in a corner in the shadows starts a hunger strike, a pacifist tries to hide his filthy fly. (I hope nobody will have the idiotic idea of organizing a *naked party*) . . . There are a lot of bald guys here. I know some who've worked for more than ten years very hard before they could take their clothes off . . . all these remarkable events are going to weigh heavily on the balance of the revolution . . . oh! hey! Here comes the courageous publisher who went further than any of the others . . . blue suit, *Rasurel* briefs, cashmere socks, he's pale, his short fingers look like maggots. He still has *foie gras* under his fingernails. Ah! here comes the slave . . . a well-dressed old man . . . I think that, by an accidental cry, we'll have to announce how temporary their situation is. Tarantulas, rats, shits, hyenas, assholes.

The pond scintillates. The sky is streaked with black bile. Sulphur vapors creeping among the ferns.

A bar. A private club, near Duke Street, Mayfair. Two characters are sipping their *gin fizzes*.

"To be frank, my dear, I place the Arab on the lowest shelf, the Wog following the dog very closely . . ."

A vision of Lawrence of Poland, riding a pig, clothed in a filthy white djellaba, entering Warsaw in triumph.

One of the latest tunes puked by the jukebox, "Suck me but don't put it in!" Scraps of conversation. I take it all in. A kind of wild madness depicting the collective unconsciousness, I make a mental note, I note quite a few things in bars, night clubs, taxis, toilets, on airplanes, on a boat, in a train, in the streets that are preferable empty.

Sloane Square, two men chat sitting on a bench. I sit down, with an innocent expression, my Sony in my pocket. Shit! Frenchmen! . . .

"Man, America is it! No fuss over there, I tell ya it's it! Very nice . . ."

"Yeah, have you been there?"

"No, but I know, I know I'm right . . ."

"Yeah, um . . . yeah . . ."

Strange guys. Blue jeans and spotted anoraks, boots, dirty sleeping bags filled with half-eaten sandwiches, silly amulets made in Hong Kong imitating Navaho motifs . . . they're looking for guys from *The Living Theater,* and be on their way (sic) . . . thin hair, straggly, greasy, crooked glasses tainted by grease and obviously a few pimples . . . They're perfect! Exactly the kind of guys I adore . . .

"I'm gonna learn Yoga, man, then I'll wait until you're connected to teach you how to play tabla, now I'm gonna show you a mantra I wrote last night, at some guy's . . ."—then they wondered for a moment where they would sleep, or eat, leafing through the London *underground* guide book . . . evoking the road to Nepal, San Francisco, Onan City *(sic)*—"Then we'll go to see thingamajig, he'll give us free tips on America" . . . a rotten transistor . . . The dean of chimpanzees died this morning stricken by a heart attack . . . a diabolical substance is motionless over Buckingham Palace, Portabello Road is buried under a tidal wave of grease spots, *to be continued* is drawn in the sky by a helicopter.

A pub, *The George* . . .

"Blacks are lazy, thieves, but, on the whole, rather nice."

"Sure, but there is no work for the English."

Those two guys groaned about Europe's Seven Wounds, pulling on the old strings of the all-knowing man in the street.

"But remember this . . ."

A telecommunication satellite station is damaged by an explosion.

"That's enough!", cried the minister. "What is this? Another revolutionary with no revolution!"

"Yes, Chief. Badly informed, therefore badly thought out."

"Shut up! Jerk! Vomit your laudanum and get to work."

"You may be familiar with me Chief."

"Give this message to the assholes, and fast!"

A ceremony around a mutilated body, larded with stab wounds. His genitals are horribly mutilated . . . Manson, whose tender passion for Bobby Beausoleil, thought the bride was too beautiful—a fashionable terrorist held forth in front of the gates of a factory, it was Sunday, there was nobody around. He had abandoned everything to militate.

Collective feelings are insinuated into the messages of futurologists.

A cargo-plane crashes on a shanty town of dilapidated caravans and old cars. Snow-covered disaffected building lots.

Political demons advance in tight rows, threatening and grotesque. All is permitted. Huge shortcuts in mondo-vision on the masses of demonstrators worldwide. All this is quite mysterious, partisans, adversaries and allies don't know what it is all about. Are they even sure they exist? In the halls of Studio Reality the Invisibles smile.

Cops surround a bloc of Housing Projects. Insupportable, brutal scenes.

A yellow fog engulfs the city.

Circumstances are made of dust.

"Let the situation rot, we've seen everything else. It's simple, those people are too far away from the system they want to combat . . . an irretrievable lateness . . . as for you, Dickhead, watch out, you can easily be replaced and recycled, ya dig?"

"Yes, Chief", answers the minister's assistant, his finest collaborator, as he likes to think . . . He clicks his heels, kneels down, opens the boss' fly and gives him a blow job . . . A global view of Dublin from a jumbo jet, a global view of Shannon, then Kennedy International Airport, New York . . . Faded photos exploding in the windows of the Gotham Book Mart, faded smoke around two thin cats playing in the dusty window of the Phoenix Bookshop . . . wind sucks the thieving shadows, sharp cries in the oven of the 60s, sexual guerilla warfare in the streets of the world. Nothing has changed. Everything is just a little sadder, a little deader.

WHITE FLOWERS ON THE SCREEN

Young homosexuals castrated by *skinheads* expelled from their gray suburbs. Pakistanis stabbed in the dark streets around Piccadilly Circus. Apartments set on fire, hippies brutalized. Two ex-paratroopers disembowel a Jamaican, stuffing his belly with garbage taken from the trash cans of a Chinese restaurant. "Here, Brillohead! Here you are stuffed with something worse than your own shit!" Later on they kidnap a young girl who hung out with a Pakistani, and fill her vagina with quick-drying cement.

Televised mud is spreading. John Wayne and Audie Murphy, The Duke manipulates platitudes with humor. Driving the Blue Fetus' khaki Rolls, he rushes toward the Cote d'Azur. Hamburger Gyp ends his days in a hotel in Seaford.

A green flash in the purple fog . . . naked, standing on the State Ship, the Prime Minister rushes towards more pleasant climates. Sexual segregation in the streets of the world.

The Pink Panther won't finish its speech, a sexist flash, red, erasing half its face. "SEXTERA", I murmured as I took a photo.

Strange sounds invading High Camden Street.

Thousands of jobless people wandered in the streets, waiting for the opening of dismal pubs.

A cinemascopic duel and bossa nova.

"Sir, I, who am not a racist, I do think the crappers should be segregated."

73

Soft music in the dimmed back-room. Red Charlotte distributed tracts.

Israeli secret agents placed bombs in a wimpy. Dead drunk Pollacks drink Javel water and bite directly into packages of frozen food. An ad: "Madam, if you have greasy hair, eat some baba mousse" another ad, "Put a little springtime in your sandwiches, buy endives" . . . "Your son takes drugs, your daughter is a prostitute, come to us for consultations, *FAMILY PLANNING JELLY ROOTS*' . . . toothpaste for dogs is sold illegally in Great Britain . . .

An extraordinary reunion. The general secretary of the Unique Party, a wounded vet and a work hero has the floor. His artificial anus plugged into a bottle of Propane gas. Two young militants stand at his side, armed with bicycle pumps in case of a breakdown or sabotage.

"Comrades, uh where are we with the Tierce? Uh uh, ah ah, the minister hasn't paid his taxes, hihihi . . . uh uh . . . comrades, uh . . . arrrhhh! But go on and pump you little shits! . . . uh! . . . Pump!"

The General secretary collapses. The undersecretary grabs the mike.

"Pump! But go on and pump!"

"Comrades we're not responsible for the thousands of young druggies who vegetate in psychiatric hospitals, and I say—Yes! We've thought of everything, education, cultural revolution, sexual revolution, counterculture, sports and leisure, cold buffets, drinking holes, crappers and pop music . . ."

"It's the fault of LSD!" cried a self-made union man.

"He's drunk! Just get that baboon the fuck out of here!"

"But he's a comrade!"

"Don't give a fuck!"

"But he's a work hero!"

Don't give a fuck! He's kicked out of the Party's control! A militant must behave, be an example . . . there are too many faggots here!"

I was of the same mind, but who am I to criticize? I was there, with an extraordinary mission for the *Insect Trust Gazette.*

Hideous images were distributed to *young adults* and to schizophrenics.

"An historic flop", I said to the Muslim representative to Blacks from North America. He nodded, spreading his little plastic rug he began his prayer. An Eskimo Guevarist representative told me: "There's no discussing with people like that!"

The cultural industry has always been influenced by military & industrial complexes, which is normal, whether it's about persona; capitalism or State capitalism, even Socialist, that's how the techniques of brain washing are abandoned in advanced capitalistic countries, the Control Organism possesses much scarier weapons than that. The imperialism of the stomach and social security have rendered pre-war techniques null and void. We're entering a golden age. "Eat, drive fast, jack off, organize your leisure, idiocy is in power!" a period some might regret, paranoia of hearts and minds.

"Where are we with the control of information, Watson?"

"I really think that we are in the majority . . ."

75

"Ah, good, and are the masses of polling following?"

"Yes, like a single man . . ."

"Perfect, Watson, perfect, well, Watson, let's have a little sniff, the State's blue cocaine . . . ah, Watson, increase the free distribution of sausages a bit, as well as wine and beer, that's very important, Watson . . . we must remain neutral."

Children are selling 'Le Cri du People' in the empty streets.

Drunk with rage and hate the police stomp cadavers.

Veterans, stoned, parade naked, tears of pride sparkling in their filthy eyes.

The nation's pupils demand the heads of the idle, of sleepwalkers and faggots. Scoundrels exploit public misery, put itching-powder in the stocks of plasma, stop ambulances to set fire to them. Official statistics explode in the cellar of the Sperm Bank.

"Give shit to those who are hungry!" I screamed in a fit of generosity.

Fifty year-old black leather jackets attack isolated passerby with syringes filled with curare.

"Now that's fine, Watson, good job, the people want information, true TV news" . . . a CEO agonizes, clobbered by a chimpanzee . . . confusion reigns in the slums of the city . . . a group of social students are ambushed . . . Her Majesty the Queen hitchhikes in Asia.

"So, when we think about it, they call us cowards" murmured a cop, on all fours, pants down, buggered by a red-headed, green-eyed sailor. Another one yells with his mouth full of come: "Ugh! Good God!

76

Where are the elite!" . . . a CIA agent high on heroin absently scratches his balls.

I was lucky to witness the raking of Sacramento by the red drag queens. At that time dwarfs stayed quietly away. Reagan leading the assault units, surrounded the vacant lots in Harlem. The idol of songs was on stage. A mini-Woodstock failure. He fiddled with his amplifier. We put TNT in his electric guitar. You should have seen the flash when he pressed the button, BANG! BANG! . . . and his expression! . . . better than napalm . . . and his pianist sizzled when he placed his feet on the pedals of his electric organ, SRRR rrrssshhhh! . . . A smell of burnt flesh and a commercial flash, some of the fans fainted, nothing much was left, his Italian boots and cuff links.

"Bravo! Bravo!" cried the police commissioner, "when I say *musicians under police protection* I'm not saying in the morgue!

Some Bangladesh partisans struck up the national anthem.

"Those people won't go far, Watson, with that kind of a song . . ."

A few scabs beat the wives of strikers. Ixca and Sally were fucking in a beet field. Suddenly Ixca found himself alone, the cock armed . . . Sally's clenched hand was disappearing in the mud . . . a few bubbles then an awful silence. Stunned, Ixca looked around him, he saw an upset sign where he could still read: "DANGER QUICKSAND".

The super Yeti and the Swami organize a competition of spiritual grimaces. Their sexual tentacles left imprints in the sand.

77

Heaven will thank you. You will thank heaven. Everyone is very polite.

The swami made a little greasy, wet sound. God doesn't need gate-keepers. Men tell a few untrue stories, that's the trouble.

Tomorrow, the vision of several million individuals will be upset by the international market of cables and video-cassettes. I won't insist on mentioning the political side of that *revolution.*

The cries of militants turn into murmurs. Ectoplasm pushes against them and sodomizes them, then fill all their orifices. Their groans and murmurs prove they like to be humiliated.

After having come for a long time in Red Charlotte's ass, an ectoplasm forced her to her knees, and plunged her tongue into the heroine's rectum and swallowed his sperm. Little by little they all dovetailed happily, dabbing their anuses with bits of cotton soaked in brilliantine.

"You'll earn your bread by the sweat of your brow" murmured the hypermarket manager.

"We will force them to make their peace with their work!" cried a student from Teachers' College who had dropped out to work in a factory and who was not used to sodomy. A young hoodlum glides up behind him and screws him in the ass. The muscles of his stomach harden, with a demented cry the hoodlum fucks his ass. The brilliant militant shudders, and his cock spews, splattering the shelf of fine lingerie. On the assembly line of programmed sodomy there were quite a few candidates. Then all the demonstrators were dominated by sexual rage. The cops distinguished themselves as soon as they lost their inhibitions. The crowd officiated actively. Unfortunately the seriousness of politics and the game took the upper hand, and ideological services repressed, with extreme violence any deviation, going along with the powers that be. To enjoy sex was forbidden. It was quite clear.

Incidents of rare violence went on for several weeks. Every day thousands of beings clinched. The cops sniffed their adversaries like passionate and jealous lovers.

No rapes to report.

Gigantic and impressive fornication. Intense effusions. Pure and exquisite emotions. All their senses were fulfilled. Some were unable to hold back their tears and their ecstatic cries.

Early in the morning violent fights restarted. In the daylight no sexual impulse preoccupied the protagonists.

Juju and Chano slept side by side near a barricade. Chano turned over, groaned, opened an eye . . . a terrible erection that he tried to forget . . . Chano put his hand between Juju's thigh who was still asleep, then he wet his fingers with saliva and wet Juju's anus, Juju moved a little, groaning he stretched his adorable ass. Chano penetrated him gently, holding onto his shoulders, slowly he moved up and down, he couldn't stop his movements.

Juju barely moved, contracting his rectal muscle, hoping Chano stayed there, and never relaxed his embrace.

Their bodies covered in sweat shone in the fog of teargas, the odor of come dominated. Chano came in Juju's ass, which contracted in the ultimate reaction, feeling the long spurts of come flood the bottom of his ass . . . In their trucks under their blankets, soldiers caress each other furtively, the smell of semen mixes with the odor of gas and tobacco. Some of the officers were troubled by the excesses.

A PROGRAMMED DREAM

The technician sprays toxic and lethal gases. The CEO shuffles a few pages and starts to speak.

"Gentlemen, the American astronauts will return in perfect shape, SKYLAB is a success. We're at the dawn of the year 2000, and our enhanced gadgets don't fight with the flow of history, besides that isn't the problem, the problem is, uh, well let's say that it is extravagant, if it be that our capitalist society that permitted the expansion of all consciousness and our trips into space" . . . applause . . . "that our society allowed the most audacious arts to infuse new blood into a whole generation, and that thousands of young people, among our finest technicians, were able to experiment with every kind of drug in spite of the uh-prohibition, well, I think that unadapted people have a right to happiness and the Freudian plus-value . . . Marxists have disgusted the youth of every country, and now we must adapt, change, and ALL that, Gentlemen, we can only go forward, with more and more freedom" . . . Applause . . . "so, I say , that those who wish to enjoy their incredible backward-ness, take no part in the democratic *brain trust*, the exercise of liberties that democracy demands will have nothing to do with their aberrant convictions and their nostalgia . . . Oh, I know that the war machine can still function, but it can't really affect us . . . even the Western proletariat loots the Third World" . . . laughter . . . exclamations . . . "Gentlemen, there will be no revolution in the sense that the stupid left wingers understand it, and I think that it is unbelievable luck for the revolutionaries, and, besides, I think they will soon realize that the bastards weren't those . . ."

"There were ants in the hearse!", exclaimed the union delegate.

"Oh, you, that's enough, go and tell that to your flocks!"

"I even wonder if there will be a few fine days for us", murmurs the Prime Minister sitting in his bathtub, contemplating his little celluloid boats.

"Those eyes undress you! Justice is done!", yells another delegate.

"I accuse!" grunts the doorman visibly drunk.

"Just the justice of the people . . .", the character hidden behind a curtain doesn't finish his sentence. A ton of sadness spreads throughout that congress. Joe Allegro, one of the principal stockholders wasn't there.

The CEO continues . . .

"Calm down, Gentlemen, calm down . . . Let's see now, what the youth market is offering us . . . but let's not take Europe into account, except for Great Britain . . . *popstars* are committing grave errors, they confuse the mud of abundance with the gold of time . . . those new myths, uh, for better or worse, hey we have our own fantasies, don't we? . . . I mean the *popstars* aren't profitable anymore . . . no more than anti-missiles, warheads with multiple heads, orbital bombs, carriers or missile interceptors, no more than the bacteriological and psychochemical offensives, only meteorological projects that provoke climatic catastrophes hold our attention . . . but will our environments resist the escalation?". . .

ACTION—general rehearsal in under-developed zones. Objective No 1 . . . who cares, they're not White . . . experimental non-violent repression on trial in urban and suburban volumes . . . ACTION . . . nothing to fear from militants and diverse groups . . . Hippies have found jobs and have grown old . . . universities, *fashions*, research, advertising, Dick Tracy, TV, etc., nothing to fear from liberated bourgeoisie, nothing to fear from western Communists . . . ACTION . . . we're going to be able to liquidate our Madison Avenue MGM and RCA stocks with the retarded Europeans . . . ACTION . . . population explosions, global segregation . . . we won't tolerate official subversion, and all that seems quite reasonable to us.

Let's not forget to emphasize vacations and leisure, that's really a revolutionary act . . . right and left wingers are under our control, those retarded minority layers are living their last minutes, let them rot . . . ACTION—no more classical repression, liberate those Blacks, all of them, quickly reclassify those suicide candidates . . . besides we have the time to see it happen.

"A little blue flower in the red flag, Sir?"

"Thanks, young man, I'm a socialist of the *belle époque* . . ."

"And what about me, I'm left wing, and I feel good in my skin . . ."

"I'm right wing who feels good in the world . . ."

"And you, young man? At your age, one feels good anywhere, no?"

"You? Yes, you!"

"I'm legitimately worried, oh, not a theoretical anxiety, no crisis, no . . . anyway, I hope it lasts . . ."

83

"A very fine statement concerning reality, my dear, remind me of your name?"

"And you, continue to campaign in my favor . . ."

"You know, there are discontented people all over . . ."

"Well, good night, I'm overjoyed, at least, you know what you're talking about . . ."

"Well, good night, let's say that we live in a world difficult to understand . . ."

"You know, a new washing machine, a new color photocopier are much more important than the riots in the ghettoes, besides, look carefully at the screen, do you see that street? Those young people singing the *International* in Paris and in Tokyo, well, the police do their job well . . . we've acquired the exercise of democracy and liberty, don't throw that unique acquisition away . . ."

"Of course, the obsessions and neuroses of individuals with collective unimportance don't interest us, not important if he takes her in the ass or in the urinal? with or without peppers? We're free, you got it?"

ACTION—a green flash pushes the travelers back into yesterday, the last stop for the managers of the revolution, dream chronicles, we didn't believe in it anymore . . . a sexual howl in the bloody trunk, silence, music, big lights in the pink window . . . We don't give a fuck about their sexual problems, here, we light up inwardly, we come or not . . . we aren't going to start over—English twilight carries an old address around, a few pissy bubbles burst in the sun—there are no surprises upon waking up . . .

A honey echo, emotion as pure as a drop of dew.

The sky unfolds its cloth. A cowboy song comes out of a jar full of mint leaves. Cassettes sing-song, televisions split, the shadow loots mirrors.

There's nothing left, we're on the brink of vacillating with neon . . . no explanation need be given to one or the other, you can't change their lives or transform their worlds against their wills . . . ACTION—recoil instinctively . . . A hanged man lifts the curtain and shits in the prompter's box, and before the three knocks reveals his stiff prick . . . a CEO shows off, stars are startled in the sexual mist . . . artists and revolutionaries become more and more indispensable to the established order—what is happening in the world? Nothing, not much, every subject haunts the Universe, mutant-clairvoyants advance—without a look at the blind terror and conformity sleepwalkers and robots go to the cashier. What more is there to say?

THE GREAT FUCK

Ray lifted Ida's legs to examine her twat. He was on his knees, caressing the plump mound covered with curly nut-colored fur. He put his hand between her thighs and gently caressed her clitoris. She disengaged herself, turned over, and lips bumped into Ray's penis who was sucking her conscientiously. Rapidly a sharp pleasure made him shudder. His prick was completely in her mouth, and he managed to return her caresses. Then he took her alternately in the butt and the cunt. They came together enjoying the same delights, discharging painfully . . . Hermione entered the room and covered them with her lips. Ida grabbed Hermione and sucked for her for a long time, shoving her tongue like a serpent in her streaming cunt. Ray didn't take long to get hard again, and he serviced Hermione the same way in the ass and cunt. Then he spread her thighs roughly, Ida took his cock between her lips, and at the same time finding Hermione's butt, she shoved two fingers in her rectum . . . then tickled her with her tongue . . . they were abundantly wet and Ray fucked Ida, her cunt swallowing his cock, Hermione caressed Ray's balls, then they came like madmen, fainting with pleasure.

The boys (when they weren't jacking off among themselves) were assaulting girls all the time. That sexual misery, and the many forms of repression, doesn't, I think, have much to do with class struggles, in spite of what they say in informed circles . . . The photocopier replaces the orgasm and Xerox brings another kind of civilization to us . . . flabby thinking is diffused by ideological services only impoverish sex and its market—pathetic symphony in the crappers of high schools and stations—a mammoth explosion shakes the planet . . . repression and transgression appear simultaneously, speech is completely shattered, unpredictable reactions begin and end in the present, and spread over events and environments . . . the dominant structures of a system that strangely resembles the one created by groups that are hostile to it . . . Death and come remain in their throats, the better and the worst are in their heads.

The Japanese cop who arrested Juju in Los Angeles was also a pianist, a pure artist floating in the sunset in Surf City.

Early morning stratus flying over nuclear installation in New Mexico.

An ignoble attack forces a national spermatic emission to flow.

ACTION—the deposed emir was jacking off in a bordello in Timbuktu, while the stoned Fedayeen shit in his oil wells. In Zurich silly Hippies demonstrated for peace—a video orgasm pushed back the neo-Nazi counter-demonstrators . . . there are dreams we don't remember, and that's a good thing . . . On the sexual battlefield of sleep, the dreamer is plunges into a bath of vapor . . . the most committed militants are never really taken seriously, especially by their adversaries . . . reactions are mixed.

ACTION—young, rather ugly and ungainly girls go door to door selling, an explanation campaign, the pill, abortion, social security, the friend of the fetus, the great zygomatic, etc . . . lesbians exhausted by street fighting, attack lonely men and emasculate

them, left wing housewives organize a faggot hunt . . .
"all this is comical and quite enervating," said a liberal
who contests the sisters' capabilities—Paulo, an
ex-motorcyclist who had become a rock singer in a
suburban nightclub, organized very special gang-
bangs with innocent girls . . . he would deflower them
with his Bic pen and cut their cracks with his
teeth—drowning in grease spots and used Kleenexes,
Paulo rushed forward and glided, yelling with
pleasure on his toboggan incrusted with dildos. Billy
Bud traveled with his sexual demonstrations packed in
a suitcase . . . grave consequences between the lines of
risky strength . . . I hummed the latest tune, "You're
dirty but you're handsome".

ACTION—a young man smoked leaning
against a billboard. Bare chest. pre-faded blue jeans
and red leather boots. Black hair cut very short. His
flabby lips were surrounded by pubic hairs. Ray felt a
little sick . . . a light breeze played in the silvery-green
eucalyptus foliage. Onan City was lit up. The Frisco
Bay, and over there, further on, Oakland, crushed by
the lights of Berkeley . . . Ray thought that, in fact and
in spite of everything, that it was better to live in New
York or in Los Angeles, even London, with the
conduction of being able to jump in a plane, every
week, and fly into the heart of the Blue Mountains, or
onto the beaches of the State of Virginia . . . Sexual
extinction and curfew, police and military patrols and
all the anxious and badly built people ready to lynch
you . . . Ray and the boy were standing on a pontoon . . .
accidentally Ray's hand touched his belly. The boy's
hand grasped his cock, and he fell on his knees, his
warm lips closed over Ray's prick, his tongue

caressing him slowly—the seagulls squawked—Ray held back, a trembling hard-on, shuddering as he stroked the shaved neck, digging further into that delicious, exciting mouth. Ray couldn't hold on any longer and he discharged in five long pulsations. The boy swallowed his burning come, groaning and suffocating. Then they stretched out on an inflatable mattress. Ray took off his blue jeans, stroking his tiny balls, as round as plums. They kissed and Ray tasted his own sperm—Another hard-on. The boy's penis was small but adequate . . . Ray jacked him off delicately and with his other hand caressed his ass, the assholes of the unknown kid dilated, retracted, and Ray took him in the ass, back and forth in the luscious scabbard. All around, young people were caressing each other, buggering, couples were fucking furiously, moaning and crying under the orange and black sky, blotted out by the San Francisco neon. Heavy waves break against the rocks and the surf came to caress the barge.

Operation "IT'S NEVER TOO LATE TO SEDUCE" . . . last reel . . . we'll never talk about it again . . . the ration of time for solitude is no longer available.

I was Ray a long time ago, straddling a piece of ice. Finished in a reanimation booth. Finished in the American zoo. Rowing in olive oil and a *hot fudge sundae,* straddling a Polaris-turd, celebrating Valentine's Day with the red dykes.

Red dimensions bursting through the haze, set the nylon landscape on fire. God tried to photograph something, like the Abyss Gang.

ASSASSINS WORK OVERTIME

Notices and small posters, *it's forbidden to throw beer cans into the barbed wire. Paint your ghettos green, Jazz up your hovels with psychedelic posters,* avenging posters were plastered on the walls of the city, along with the usual publicity, so subversive and demented.

A gigantic prick pierces the clouds and showers the city with cosmic sperm, an intergalactic anus defecates on the creations of man.

People fight in the streets.

There is obviously another solution, Stoned Intersection, a shabby hotel room, an unmade bed, greenish sheets, sachets of heroin, spoons, syringes, matchbooks, cotton balls, speed and barbiturates . . . all that shit spread out on the bed . . . I smoked a bit, I had a few *bennies,* and I left . . . in a bar I drank five or six Vodka martinis . . . I felt better . . . I could no longer look at those bits of blood-stained cotton, those eye-droppers full of coagulated resin, those filthy needles, I could no longer see those guys and those girls, nor—the hell of heroin, coma, cramps, gray flashes stirred inside bubbles, the withered, pierced veins under your abscessed flesh—if we could only use a telecommunication satellite to wholly film and project at random the arrival of bubbles, *overdose fixes,* and the thousands of *junkies* in a single flash, any old pad, on any old continent, in any old high school can, in any old prison . . . ACTION—I see a guy getting a fix in San Miguel, the needle trembled, the great mondo vision shot, and all the maniacal mythology of the universe of drugs . . . everyone should know that . . . Nothing happens, nothing in that universe, as soon as that filth has hooked you for good . . . five tons of rotten heroin is consumed in the USA in a year, poisoned LSD, over-priced grass is trafficked, murderous amphetamines, synthetic alcohol . . . a gray scream in the cold dawn where a thousand transparent silhouettes vacillate. The leprous anxiety emerging from the fog laden with metallic dust, a vague shock in the gelatin, shattered multicolored neon swimming in black blood, desolate and sinister zones of survival and panic, sticky wrinkles, slimy clots of sadness, a vague shock, the embers fry you vertically. If it tempts you, amuses you, engulfs you now in the Snow Subway, in the artificial dawn soaked by the blood of thousands of *junkies* bursting into torches, those thousands of suffering people who have no stories to tell, like Murphy and Floyd, dead for such a long time, with Skag and Jones, officially lying in the morgue for little powder mixed by Mol & Mort . . . I left that shabby bar and I smoked two joints in the parking lot. Then I took a taxi.

Like many people Doctor Rubin was undecided and troubled.

A rock group, *The Fat Flower,* and the demonologists of the Pentagon were dazzled by a porn *lightshow* staged by *THE Wet Dykes.*

A tear on the screen—the actor Pierre Clement is condemned by an Italian tribunal for usage and possession of drugs, the funeral of a Catholic priest in Ireland, Ginsberg and Ferlinghetti make a stopover in Honolulu, President Nixon stops over in Alaska, fights in Paris, Milan and Rome, John Sinclair is freed, wave

92

of arrests in the countries in the East, murderous fights between Palestinians and Israelis, clamp of tension over the whole planet, a Soviet poet leaves a psychiatric hospital, declared *cured* by the authorities—in the minds of one and the other all the battles were either won or lost, their demanding formulas chase reality.

A soulless doll passes in front of the automatic distributor of condoms, two guys argue about a parking spot.

Images created by ideological services experts lean on a network of contradictions. Once again I was right, and so were you. A network of *absurdities,* as some consumers might say, consumers who have views about everything and nothing, like you and me . . . As soon as they organize your leisure they're persuaded that they have freed you. A rebel in a coma speaks to us of the inconsequence of democracy. "I don't know anything and don't want to know," he repeats fiddling with his paint bomb.

The Wet Mops, a symphonic orchestra attacks the first measure of *Kibbutz Flower.*

"Assassins work overtime!"

A veteran, tied onto his emergency chamber pot with security belt and all, cries out:

"Let our dead sleep in peace!"

A gray and brown rainbow, large flakes of grated cheese fall. Operation 'GAMMA SUCCESS GUARANTEED', cops and demonstrators are absorbed by electromagnetic vibrations and plunge into infrared and ultraviolet.

Chromatic information passed under the noses of a generation too preoccupied with choosing clothes at the Oriental Pearl. The information agents didn't have much to do, if not to film, tape, classify and transmit. The electric activities of poets were drowned in adrenalin, they felt no dangers for the established order. (It was sad to see them talk gibberish on stage, holding greasy bits of paper in their hands, sputtering in mikes smeared with Dijon mustard, sad, in spite of total consciousness and the Immense Trip they are incapable of explaining to the world in which they find themselves) . . . it pleases me to see those guys embark on a pierced raft for a long cruise . . .

ACTION—the Sperm Hotel, Chelsea . . . artists, militants, dealers, CIA and FBI agents, crazies, Puerto Rican whores, and Cuban drug dealers . . . the situation deteriorated quickly, the *belle époque* was over, musicians went elsewhere, everyone was perfect . . . rapes, murders, break-ins, regrettable incidents, absolutely disgusting people took care of business . . . At all times New York was considered to be a dangerous city, like all the other large American cities.

A pink taste in that cruel glance. A vision of the world transcends pinball machines on 42nd Street. The old film must be decoded. An intestinal occlusion that tends to replace any important cultural contribution . . . The CIA agent, long hair, black shades, etc., at the bar, exploiting Chibas' gestures . . . the bursting open of an old film and of conscience is the starting point of the arrival of blocs of association, that return at random, after the seen and the heard, hoping to make you smile.

A jazzy goodbye buried in the jukebox in this filthy dive, the El Coyote . . . all that ruins memories, a metabolic shock caresses twilight, like a spurt of sperm falling in flakes on the worn bath mat, a soft noise, a gray sound.

As soon as you exaggerate and you take your desires for realities you start to invent. We catch all the signs drifting among reflections of waves whispering on the edges of clouds.

"You're making fun of my body!" cried Lola Pozo as she readjusted her veil. That poor drag-queen was aging badly, her acting clothes were faded.

That day, returning from Las Vegas, I noticed that the old Beatniks were resurfacing again, betting on the Hippy market, that all the crazy exiled avant-garde of the 50s were escaping from the Jewish psychoanalysts' waiting rooms, and that it was really touching bottom . . . a neurotic and romantic wind blew in the halls of the hotel, not to mention the bad smells. Daily low blood pressure, filthy beings, eroded by rages and hatreds, and the hideous sounds of 23rd Street . . . things go so fast that questions and answers telescope, and that double vision turns into impenetrable dullness . . . the hideous images rise in your field of vision.

ACTION—for a week now, professor Tchou Wrong reads and rereads the Supreme Public Servant's latest book. He always worked cold and practiced acupuncture by correspondence. He operated cold, scalpel in his left hand, the little red book in his right one. Obviously his successes were very limited—song week in Peking went on without incident—Paris and London were crushed by grayness, and the Soviet Union not yet hypnotized by Nixon seriously thought of joining the Common

Market . . . here, assassins were working overtime.

ACTION—4 pm, the lounge at the Chelsea Hotel . . . *they* entered the lounge completely stoned, armed to the teeth, brandishing the Pink October pickets . . . they stank of ether, rubbing alcohol, some were tripping, THC and super pot, most of them were high on amphetamines . . . originally they wanted a Housing Project for themselves on 9th Ave, but they decided to start with the Chelsea Hotel and the YMCA swimming pool . . . automatic-gun shots between the legs of bathers lying under tanning lamps, grenades thrown into the pool . . . hundreds of bloody bodies floated in the water, some hung on diving boards . . . pale green-blue water turning red, purple . . . bullet-riddled bodies covered with grenade shards lay on the steps leading to the steam-baths, *Fag Cruise Row* . . . life-guards were nailed onto the doors of cabins . . . mirrors were shattered, grenades were thrown into elevator shafts like rosary beads . . . puddles of blood everywhere . . . *they* entered the hotel lobby— pictures painted by masters, bought cheap, were riddled with bullets, telephone operators were killed on their chairs, the manager was hacked to death . . . the black doormen were chased into the cellars of the hotel by a small group armed with hatchets and electric saws . . . maids were murdered on the staircase—the doors of rooms were bashed in, dynamited, a rock group was machine-gunned while rehearsing, the singer bends his knees swallowing his last tremolo, the drummer takes burning flames in his eyes, fire licks away his face, another group is armed with flame-throwers . . . people are killed in their bathtubs, in their showers, sitting on their toilets, some in their beds, others are

thrown out of the windows . . . children are not spared .
. . some try to escape onto the balcony, terraces,
emergency stairs, hanging gardens, etc—shots tear
through chests, stomachs, backs, tear off heads,
marmalades of brains on the walls, guts . . . An artist
falls holding his palette, a guy finishing his best-seller
(*I was a Hippy before the letter)* falls on his nose on his
typewriter, burst apart, twisted, smoking . . . the old
couturier and his dogs and his chicks are axed in the
hall, the Caucasian poetess opens her big mouth for
the last time while her Cuban lover rolls like a gazelle
against the wall . . . white nylon carpets are covered in
blood . . . artists offer money to the killers, models and
actresses offer their bodies to the sanguinary
hoodlums . . . then it was the turn of the bar and the
restaurant the *El Coyote* . . . I rejoiced over the fate of
the bar and the restaurant, I liked it . . . An
Italian-American, Number 1 on the Hit Parade was
gunned down holding his orange juice . . . the Spanish
waiters had collapsed in the straw and Vagina Soufflé . .
. "Ole! Ole!" I screamed . . .

"You dig, people don't think, they only repeat
what they hear" . . .

"I didn't make you say that . . ."

"Antonio! fucks! Give me the wine chart!"

"¡Si Senor!"

An incident among so many others—and two
steps away, at *Madison Square Garden,* the mentally
handicapped people of the American Communist
Party claim that Socialism is on the march—Maurice
Chevalier arrives on the Concord which will later be
turned back, a forced landing in Switzerland . . . Then
the swami throws his lighted cigarette into the mouth

97

of the semi-artist who cries: "Good God! I don't fear anything you old blow-jobber!" . . . a German face-lifter bursts into tears, he just missed his thirteenth head transplant.

TOBOGGAN-ARCHIVE

*TRANS-FUCK EXPRESS. CENTER FOR LIFE &
DEATH.*
I had noted: *Nixon spreads skag shit bugs
VD & Death,* the great news headlines slip along
endlessly.
Toboggan-Archive, an echo-photo of another
world. This morning the dew liked to bite. Supreme
Cosmos sauce . . . I listen to the propellers riddle my
silence. A mauve sun devours what is left of my sky.
Forests speak that language.
(You don't go from love to tenderness like that,
wind is needed. Especially when roses threaten the
stars and want to swallow the Ocean) . . . pearls dance
in cats' eyes . . . rain is never careful, it's no longer in
the sky, the moon descends on her silent track.
A few tatters of light play on the walls. Birds
defy the hurricane.
(We saw you behind an electric guitar, with an
intelligible variable sound). In spurts the coffee pot
moans.
Another blue plane high up in the sky.
A blood clot darkens the Ocean.
Faded flowers in the fireplace.
Cymbals, gongs, tambourines.
Twilight's redness teases the white grass. God
is after the slightest information. Traces of winter have
remained in the transistors of innocence. A finger of
shadows in the grass. Guerilla warfare of nerves and
charms.

Somewhat arbitrarily we live in the resonances of yesterday. The dead let themselves be buggered in silence, in front of the mirror, or in an invisible trunk . . . the others, who keep cool, simper and chatter, charming in their little flowered dresses. Nothing is revolutionized anymore. Radioactive rain falls gently. I have contemplated the stars for a long time, breathing the odor of wild mint, raspberries and strawberries. Owls have settled in the trees around the pond. Wild cats growl on the edge of the path. The forest's shadow transmits lovely chords—The end of the War of the Roses, a few traces under old stones—worlds unwind, continents collide. An upholsterer's tack in the planet's heart. And the wind puts these events in storage . . . The man from the North lights up in space and time . . . we express ourselves miraculously, we're here, with programmed death . . . no Russian, American or Chinese version, only the livable and unlivable exist . . . it's clear and easy to choose . . . there is only one vision that is opposed to the manipulations of the media. Enemy voices consume as much as we do—we blossom in ossuary-pits—so? To heal the burn, in a showered neon lights, stars and sperm. The brain's beak is rusty, rotten, things end in cowardly laughter, on the shaky stairway of thought, and I still hear that laughter seizing the ashes of Janis Joplin, Neal Cassidy, Jimi Hendrix, Brian Jones and Jim Morrison . . . black cold is a great block of colors . . . the landscape can still change, as well as the whole planet and all of life.

The streams are frozen.

Magicians advance across the fields. There will never be enough music or silence.

No gross simplification. We express ourselves. We communicate so as to better understand our environments and our personal spaces. Often, we don't know what to do with our freedoms and our powers. If all our subversive or *nihilistic* action . . . the violence of robots and hamburger-beings is responsible for all that . . . it isn't by chance that their rages are concentrated on Doctor Leary and pot smokers. Empty streets still pretend to believe in reality . . . vomit of dirty hands used to bear arms . . . wind is perhaps the pivot of the plot of all the colors, the televised colors of the global village decapitate every ideology. You will find none of that in either newspapers or books.

Doing nothing, the achievement of all poetry—the sky crackles in children's eyes—surely you're not going to live on the finger prints of a generation?

Speech is a green banana, penetrated like a dog on the head cheese canapé. Anxious, unstable men manipulate God's toys . . . it's hard to be dead, and it never ends . . . but it's difficult indeed to live . . . the Enchanter has gone by . . . the electrified verb is in the jukebox.

A pure love contract explodes. Native erections in the Bayous. The trees moved last night, and I saw an eye drown in chewing gum . . . wood, whiter than snow, crackles in the fireplace, shadows hanging onto distant voices, above phallic peninsulas, a draft of air in the silent majority's fat ass . . . your eyes are spattered with mouths glued onto napalm, the Magician guides the tide of black stars.

The White God turns bodies into walls, streets into dumps, and starving seagulls devour Black heavens and the silent traces of these millennia. The airport was empty. A few white roses abandoned on a cart. Men are dozing in the bar. Insomnia wrecks the last words of a landscape that will never breathe again. The hairs of silence have nothing more to say.

The four veins of the Atlantic have been bled. The Pacific has shaken the sheets of adventure. Motors sleep between the thighs of girls and boys.

Catatonic neon freezes in the middle of that mandala. Blood fluids buried itself in the chimney.

I'm absorbed by doing nothing.

Love given up, civilized hatred . . . where are you, beautiful children? . . . God's madmen are a few heads taller than you, Walden may be at your heart's gate but morning glory seeds haven't extinguished the fires of summer. As the days go by blood's song rises to the sky, the wind's mouth swallows the come of computers, all the colors of the rainbow die on the windshield.

Never forget that walls are greedy like the sounds that circulate in the streets of the world. The sun's flowers stammer and stutter.

TV-Philter, specters, everything is related to table-tennis. Sociologist-sewer cleaners predict the future. We meditate, we play with ourselves, we climb trees, we bark, we babble, we absorb a smile that never leaves us, and we brandish our forks. Today I don't know the positions of the stars (but, instinctively I know that the weather will be fine), I contemplate a livable horizon (I know that we won't all escape violence or injustice), much information broadcast on

102

TV in color floods our brains. Feeling-wise we may be the most poorly equipped of all the animals. Electric and chemical energy program our gestures and our thoughts.

THE SHIP OF FOOLS

A hideous crowd is moving forward. Thousands of beings are dragging themselves on their asses. The crowd is panhandling souls. Descent into hell . . . (at times I fume, I flip out, I do foolish things, and it chagrins me) . . . the drums of memory don't beat anymore for dead souls, naked souls invent simple music, very inspirational . . . an arrow carries our tears away. Tonight the trees are weeping. Language mixes up every expression. Your *domain* like mine is made up of scraps, and I am obliged to use some kind of punctuation, a strict order from my publisher and his henchmen . . . curdled blood on the windowpane, snots, spatterings of brains, blue and white roses . . . a dawn ceremony.

We'll eventually see what they'll say in the transparencies. Silence caresses their sexual stumps.

The world has taken on a disquieting meaning. God has made a success of it. Heaven thanks you. Souls throw themselves onto Madison Avenue's psychedelic frying pan. Neon is budding, pukes, Times Square, Piccadilly Circus, The Golden Gate Bridge, Big Sur, and the film unreels . . . (of course, robots and controllers have their reasons that are *beyond* our comprehension, do you jerks know what's going on right before your eyes, backstage? No. Well, of course, you're fools. Don't ask the Biological Crusher Woman nor the Dialectic Slime. Only wild flowers have answers to everything) . . . Am I here? Surrounded by filthy beings from another planet and the entrails of the earth, man-fiber! . . . fourteen years, that's what's left after the *experts,* after me, nothing but a desert! . . . I'm here, a flipped out Spirou, dawn's saw teeth pull me out of my sleep.

Juju spied the sexy message and forestalled the massage, a vibrant erection in the warmth of the early morning. Ixca grabbed Juju's prick and sucked it. Juju held Ixca's head in his hands, stuffing his fingers into his ears . . . Peter was jacking off in front of the mirror groaning . . . Juju pushed deeper in Ixca's mouth, hit his throat, came violently, shaken by the light. A stream of come flowed from Ixca's nostrils, like lava. The sexy message bombarded thought. In the heart of a sexual jungle, in unknown territory, the invasion of the *limbs-anus-vagina-tongue-fingers-mouths* machines—the wind shrieked obscenities to the phallic radars that bordered the highway—the massacre of chromosomes on Cielo Drive, a horrible sexual spectacle, parano-schizo . . . tele-info and cultural animation . . . a horse-hair glove bristling with electric needles ransacks the old faggot's ass . . . carnivorous lotus flowers . . . the din overshadows and floods reality, phantoms and specters on the move, tele-manipulation by demons—that is how politics quickly turn into a bloody, absurd, unholy mess—a jet of sperm spatters the maps at headquarters . . . the Head of State takes off his trousers and his briefs . . . a short cock, knotty, huge flabby balls covered with red hairs . . . that unbelievable prick vanished between the thighs of the matron of the Soviet Pentagon—we are now in a drugstore on 14th St., a dark-skinned Hispanic crowd . . . a young Puerto Rican unbuckles his belt, a customer smiles stupidly and expertly slicks the young man's eyebrows . . . people come and go . . . the customer slips a nicotine-stained finger into the zipper, the young man was wearing no underwear . . . the customer manipulates the minuscule sex—an odor of hamburgers and brilliantine mixes with the innocent games of the streets of New York blessed by neon lights—Sperm Hotel on 23rd St . . . a Black man pushes his cock into the sheath of a young man from Montana, as blond as a nordic ruin . . . a phony copy of James Dean is immobilized over the bed—The Black man fucks like a madman, the boy ejaculates, groaning, on the bedspread . . . Tijuana, a sperm transfusion in a Mexican clinic . . . ignoble dealing in front of the Sperm Bank—junkies selling their blood . . . the tragedy is described by a thousand different sounds made by men on the city walls and in the subway—diverse and monstrous noises, shocks, murders, rapes, aggressions, scarves of slimy fog caressing the effeminate adolescents . . . Exhausted by the New York heat, naked on his bed, Ray was leafing through *Silver Surfer.* Juju and Ixca played cards and smoked. Juju put his hand on Ixca's rigid sex. Ida and Hermione were taking a shower . . . groans of pleasure and purring could be heard from the air conditioning vent . . . Juju smiled, swallowing his smoke. Ixca knelt and buried his head between Juju's thighs, moistening Juju's gland with saliva, then he lay down and Juju penetrated him—a vague erection bothered me for a moment, then I fell asleep—Ida and Hermione, naked on the bed, smoking, whispering, giggling . . . on the tape-machine *Little Pointed Head* was playing . . . Hermione was massaging my cock and my balls, I could hear Juju and Ixca moaning . . . I had a hard-on . . . my prick vibrated under Ida's cool fingers . . . Ida licked my balls and plunged her tongue into my ass—Hermione rose like a balloon and squashed her pussy on my mouth, Ida sucked me—a silvery robot burst into the room . . . a black hood covered his head, a silvery robot shining in the dim light with thin strips of pink neon surrounding his transitory, abnormally luscious under his electric flesh . . . Ida manipulated the neon zipper and pulled out his genitals . . . a complex assemblage of wires and welds ran from the extremity of his penis at the base of his sky-blue kapok balls that disappeared in the metallic carcass—epidermic reactions in the jukebox at the Electric Circus. With Maria Sativa we lead the robot to Allen's home in the country—Peter and John destroyed all his batteries and his electronic brain when they had the wild idea of putting a broom stick up his ass.

Very early in the morning, Allen and I went to bathe in the pond, on the edge of the forest of charms. We could talk quietly as we swam. Gregory and Ray Bremser were stretched out under a magnificent maple tree, they squabbled and shouted. Miles, in the middle of his electronic equipment, taped and classified fifteen years of oral poetry and bop prosody . . . Peter was in the bathroom with his pig that he washed three times a day . . . with Allen and Mary we crossed the fields, crushing wild strawberries, and at night sitting on the top of the hill, we watched the fireflies and the stars.

Allen, fucking a sacred cow, Peter impaled on a stoned *shaddu's* prick, Uncle Fudge tracking the young mothers to milk them savagely—elsewhere some extremists of every sort tried to grasp a wavering power—the wounded robot stroked his sex, and

108

managed, just the same, thanks to an emergency radar to get sodomized by about fifty Hells Angels, while John put on his evening gown, stuck an eggplant up his ass . . . Gregory, sick, drunk, ranted about the misdemeanors of Jewish homosexuality—Back in New York, the Sperm Hotel . . . evening papers were strewn all over the sidewalks, old Black winos begged—a young ephebe was having his nipples pierced, turquoise rings were placed on them—boys and girls copulated in the swimming pool . . . Harry, the Magician exhibited himself for the first time in twenty years . . . women fled screaming—sexual ricochets on the blue screen hanging above the pool at the YMCA . . . An electronic Raga, Mantra, the gongs of violence were quiet—back in Big Sur, at a *star's* house . . . Sally and Sinbad were fucking, Ixca and Juju were endlessly assfucking, mouths, twats, asses, pricks, that Norman filmed, vibrators hanging off shoulders—night highway and myriads of erections . . . Allen straddled a monstrous dong, flying over Tangier, Bill Grey chased Arab faggots brandishing his smoking P.38 . . . pornographic pink pages on the highway . . . neon saw beautiful landscapes transfigured, but the angels barked in the sky, the angels aren't happy, and this will drag many beings on the path to death, we must send a registered letter to God, right away . . . dawn in mourning the wind mentions—water dreams as it shoulders the clouds, God jumps out of bed, slips into his cloud-skin briefs, bursts out laughing and has fun—English twilight always drags an old address along.

DEATH ECHO FILES, TAPE YOUR OWN DEATH TV—hi guys! A salute to you, Neal! Good day

Kerouac! Hello Ed! Tom Clark! Ted Berrigan! John Wieners! Hi Brautigan! Giorno! Tom Vetch! Gary Snyder! Goodnight Tom Wolfe! Goodnight McClure! Hello Richard Fariña!—echoes and sprays, clouds broken by winters' double-bass—cold's eye has gone mad, memory's cotton burns—Land's End, *The Last Frontier*, Big Sur's fabulous wind and the Great Plains bring us a few rumors, night flowers eat under water.

Fire dances with white birches. Broken moons weep for Fire-Satan. Moloch's hideous face weighs anchor in the polyester and aluminum streets. Vertical and static cities have signed their death sentences. Blond mist hangs onto sand—High tide digs up the secrets of men—the Planet no longer juggles with the stars.

COCA NEON KAMERA SUTRA

"Julio Navarro invert your field of gravity, top secret" . . . we sniff danger from a distance. Psycho-explosion, operation *SUCK*, and sparks spurt from our fingers.

WUUUuuuu! Whup! WrrrRRRoooOOOO! Phut! Thock!

The forces of evil go wild. Signal and posters all over the place: *"Mason-Nixon Line"*, *"Amor Club Buncha Fags"*, *"No Blacks allowed"* . . . I feel that something is wrong . . . with the doses we've ingested we can never remain on this planet . . . submerged by three billion Wogs, asphyxiated your own garbage and our cataracts of words and images.

Splat! Szatatt! Yech! Kapow! . . . an electric sign, *"Fuck the Pope! Central Office Building"*, *Izzy Michel and Ziggy Stardust* hiccupped . . . Thwipp! . . . a comet is needed to catch up with those yo-yos.

The bomb will explode in a few seconds, and the world will know that we are the most powerful team of transvestites of all times. Obviously the thing is more serious than predicted. But we insist on doing our job, and it won't be a smell of apocalypse that will stop us . . . we find ourselves in front of a bay window with walking cadavers, Izzy Michel still has the strength to weep and play the clown. Modesty Blaise, wants to be toyed with by an extraterrestrial above all. How can we go through these walls? . . . it will be necessary to kill time's shadow . . . Izzy Michel was a victim of his own arrogance, he wanted to go to heaven. A panic film has already disfigured him.

111

Joe Verminex composed the music of "The Young Girl With The Parasol" in front of the sink. Oblivion's scream drifting in the streets of a dead city, *A Land of Wonders,* "The Solid Bourgeois Cooking", and another tango in Paris—my nerves' soul and the same old electric typewriter—words twinkle *DESTINY, POSTERITY, FUTURE*—inertia, boredom has welded the live world, as soon as someone remembers someone or some- thing it means he has not loved well—as soon as a being is animated and loved he discovers insubordination, that's when circumstances take revenge. Images, fantasies, frozen intersections, tragic autobiographies, etc. . . . and events that become the objects of passionate, idiotic comments. Is any of that necessary? Possible? If yes or no, then why? Dreamed of Warhol and Truman Capote . . . "Mr. "C" what is man's basic drama?" . . . neurotic perspective over Brighton, operation *"The Tadpole And the Fetus"* . . . those amalgams of information don't impress me, my necktie yields to the loud-speaker, an unknown pleasure of someone who has never been able to express himself publicly. The Assassin's Tango . . . the victim's blood reddening the horizon . . . the dead gods rush into the void.

Fire-spitting clouds. The heavens discolored by cosmic delights.

Joe Verminex plays dead wrapped in silence.

Rumor-blocs and events, born yesterday to fill today and tomorrow. The spectators feed on social placenta, no one wants to untie the knots, no one wants to cross the margin-frontiers, operation *"Slimy Alexandrines & Dumb Sonnets."*

We're in this domain of typewriters and

112

computers. We're on earth, prisoners of mental reservations and sentiments. More and more fools according to the laws of chance. The visibility explodes. The raw sounds of cities are ambushed in Willie Lee's hat. Specters blubber. The astronauts soar in the huge sky. The cosmic ship is an angelic flower. Operation *"Blood & Gold."* The sexual proletariat's ambitions are changing. The sexual message is a talking clock, a time zone, a gadget you may even find in heaven. Anyway, if you are on board a cloud, don't unscrew the time capsule.

Operation *"No Objective and no Foundation"*. The lonely throngs are having sexual hunger pangs. It's hard to measure the danger. Those slimy throngs are on the side of the alliance of sentences. Operation *"Sperm and White Gloves"*, Joe Verminex, the Sea Greyhound insures his bone head for a few million dollars. Operation *"It's Poetic but Expensive,"* Operation *"God Knows who!"*—we're plugged in and we bark, blood circulated in the echo room, we're in straitjackets, and the writing-wonder goes back to work. We won't be able to resist the crossbreeding of words. We already have gray times—torn figures and broken lines of association.

And death that takes all will not return . . .

The unbearably devastating daily grind, the mechanical ballet, the electronic legend, death-TV, the spontaneity of technological ideologies and everything in the sewer . . . contradictions don't astonish me anymore, I have other dreams to live through . . . we have to *do,* as if we were alone in the world, *do and undo,* acting in favor of solitude—we're haunted by the question of truth, it's often ugly and ragged—nausea

113

and grief, despair, indifference, stupor. No abstraction can be made of them.

The weather is fine. Day is breaking. Flowers are waving at me. Birds and squirrels are playing dominos.

The weather is fine. Daylight locks us in.

The sick screen is flushed with color, crackles, we see Nixon, Pompidou, Brezhnev, Asshole & Co . . . a flat, livid face rehashed yesterday's and today's news . . . a state of supreme indifference dominates, we find our goods all over.

In every scream there is a taste of sky.

THE LAST BULLET "IN EACH SCREAM THERE IS A TASTE OF SKY"

The Universe is starved for life. We're here, in front of the video library of the Universe, in the middle of flames and flowers. The Brain Police have invaded every cerebral territory. We're thoughtlessly confronting the reasons that permit us to exist, where the dead gods were sitting . . . vibrations and the harmonies are rooted in environment-space and program the management of cerebral territories.

Operation *"The Future of Mankind."* Political manipulations, appropriate propaganda, bureaucratic and technological dictatorship, all this exceeding the left or the right, relics of the XIXth century, slime made up of slogans, archetypes and clichés, televised smears.

If we want to survive we only have two choices.

a/ ASTRONAUT.

b/ AQUANAUT.

And it may all depend on mutations caused by Sexual Affairs.

A few half-witted hippies swim in the Vision Ditch, it's always the same story, the Gospel According to Your Neighbors or to each His Own Truth, Beards and Hair, etc. . . . operation *"To Not Mow The Lawn . . ."* That is the firing of a writer . . . it's not a question of landing in Venice with a cardboard suitcase . . . The technician writes the word DEATH on the screen . . . Rumors from the city tell us nothing at all. The madness of mankind is mentioned a lot, "drugs" and sexuality, they mix everything up, and only the blind repression that strikes us is the same.

115

Cold or passionate, the technician knows what *talking* means in police language. We're in Orange Studio and we send sexy messages to distant galaxies. There's no doubt, all these messages come from space, and we're here, in time, we're not in space. We're all old Death TV.

Black lianas, coppery anemones . . . vertigo . . . the letter and the spirit of the law . . . it was yesterday . . . I disappear in a burst of laughter. "Linguistic Divorce SVP." Extra-divine version of the historic nightmare. The event, man, chance, necessity, the global village, television turned into an outcry, vision, the soul.

We yield very quickly, we listen to space.

The old world is behind us, maybe, maybe not.

We're going to write in lights, in radio-waves, in radar-waves, and we'll leave time. I get on my ergonomic bicycle, and free-wheeling I race to the House of Sausage. I benefit by a general impression. The SS in skirts organize the operation *"Renewal of the dialogue We're Going to Free the Lawn And Chop Off The Balls of Faggots,"* in fact it concerns operation *"Soup A La Grimace"* . . . on the moving sidewalks, mute, stunned, thousands of diplomaed citizens, recessed, give themselves up to work, GIVE THEMSELVES UP, what an expression! . . . what promiscuity . . . they advance, stumble, gesticulate, fight, crawl, and they endure that silence because they are all alike. Ugly smiles of several generations. And the rest emerges, as if by magic.

A taxi crammed with dwarfs rushes towards the subway entrance.

That was yesterday.

Some claim that traveling is useless—I don't claim a thing, I don't even take sides—I have no solution to propose to you, not even a suggestion, just complete indifference . . . you wander in a forest of fists with no hands, with phantoms . . . Operation *"Nitty Gritty Dirt Band"* . . . a thorny question . . . to create another paranoia, an antisocial, unadapted schizophrenic being, by affirming that your reality is the only reality . . . metabolism reversed, sabotaged, muddles and firedamp explosions . . . Operation *speed freak* . . . I press on the handle held together by nylon threads and I open fire on the dwarfs and the sexual proletariat, and all those dressed in their Tarzan costumes.

"Watch Out! To your stations! . . . we're going to change galaxies."

"We're in our own bubble, we're entering sub-space, lower your heads and fasten your belts . . ."

WHAP! ZONK! SLOOooooosssh!

"You look sad."

"I dread catastrophe, the ecoshit, you know?"

"I only dread that the duo love . . ."

KRRRIIiiiissss! CRASH! BANG! WOOW!

"Good Lord! That voice . . ."

"Get lost! Shut up, punk! Crapman was here . . ."

"Silence, amigo, if you feel like laughing, tickle yourself . . ."

"Flash Gordon! You, here!!!"

"You miserable cocksucker! What can your power do against the Controller's?"

"Eat shit, you motherfucking cunt!"

Fasten your seatbelts! According to my calculations the planet we're looking for is straight ahead . . ."

"Tough shit! Gosh!"

GURK! YUK! MEAP! MEAP! MEAP!

Operation *"Night of the drums"*, rendezvous at Pompano Piazza, keep left please. Operation *"Fascist Follies"* . . . "We're almost there, unfasten your seatbelts" . . . CRASH! TWANG! THOK! VRRRrrrrooooooooooo! . . .

I'm drowning in a secret smoke. Neon cracks as soon as you stir the metabolic ashes of the planet. Neon strangles itself. NEON-GALLOWS IN THE STREETS OF THE WORLD.

(I'm not comfortable in Van Gogh's shoes, nor Anne Frank's and those of Pope Jeanne's. I've never felt comfortable in the shoes of others)—that was yesterday . . . today it's a matter of coming to the surface . . . I don't feel comfortable in the middle of these spurts of community living. In truth, I don't feel comfortable anywhere, except here at times, and in Big Sur. But *there are the shit-makers* . . . I don't have to explain, but I'm willing to exchange a future fag for a heartbreaker.

A firing-squad festival, also a psychiatric hospital one, concentration camps too, model prisons and pilot factories . . . an orthodox brain, an autonomous prick and a cosmic grimace . . . it's a matter of fertilizing space, of getting away from the walls where we dreamed for such a long time. Kilometers of noises. The songs are heard all over. The sky's spare parts have gone on a honeymoon. Prophecies come out of the jukebox and sing inside the almond-night. Neon has lost its strength.

There were many of us on the cotton reef.

John Deeper doesn't answer anymore.

Flash-echoes in the streets of the world.

A DROP OF SKY IN A SONG

The Cosmic Hooker, frustrated and joyless, accepted to meet the Unknown Banana. She exchanged a few practical details concerning the operation *"We're not shy at all."*

The Electric Phantom of Technopolis, paradise and battlefield, as I've already mentioned . . . On the walls, or on a wall of pink paper roses, between two blizzards, during that black spring, deploying the Polaroid rainbow over the reality-pit . . . there where musicians land, in the scream of a needle . . . jostling the cop-excrement.

A billboard, COCA NEON, and you find yourself in total reality.

Semantic traps are dangerous. You can always ask—A flower, a blue flame, a *trip* and it's over, you come back or not. It's happened—we're inside our own bubbles, irresponsible, and frequency-souls howl, and the Cosmic Hooker standing in front of the pinball machines of the past seduces the co-pilot . . . I see it all from the interior, towards the unknown . . . and the gentle typewriter yells: *SAUVE QUI PEUT!!!* . . . Images of cities burning on an ordinary pillow, there where a whole generation was sitting. Death TV is new skin.

The naked and the dead, frozen on the background of a dazzling cipher, life, between two worlds, you could be mistaken . . . language stairways, Mexico, so white, between two silences . . . we hand you VCRs and the riddled arms, we know that you have nothing to live for, that you're frozen, wandering

119

in this old world, closed, voiceless, it was yesterday, DESESPERANTO . . . suffering installs its transistors.

Who is talking here?

The electrocuted articulate one or the colorless length of a scream?

I went through someone in the disorder of skins.

Dumped with all the bubbles, steamed, with seaweed faces and old photos, along with invisible intersections.

A corner of blue sky . . . the dream abyss.

Were you ever in the Sperm Hotel? In contact with the cold . . . a cure, don't you think? . . . to eat at night with a rootless drifting body, with embryo goiters . . .

Operation *"The Vice Of Living"*. Space maneuvers in a swimming pool—orange mist, TV antennae shine on the musical urinal—sexual odors on the windshield, distant explosions, sexual hostages . . . our world is swaying with dimmers (one day, you'll understand what *atomized* means) . . . On the screen, burned faces and colorless toys.

The dwarf wanted the floor. We sent them a specter. Then cameras let the toxic gases out.

Assemblages of something . . . Operation *"What's Said About It"* . . . a dumb smile between your legs . . . jumbles, dreams, all sorts of worlds to vomit, KARMA TANTRIC DIABLO. *Black and red ants unite* . . . the invisible insurrection of millions of brains of the Gray Generation.

Some dwarfs dressed in blisters patrolled the streets.

It was yesterday. It was tomorrow.

It was obvious.

The blue of the earth filled the screen.

The astronauts are very calm.

The planet's sex, turns over by itself. An alarm signal whistles at the void—on the arm of absence that *lightshow* widens consciousness—yesterday, the dream was erased, the war was over . . . today you are the heads of the publicity of your paranoia . . . WORDS AMONG THE IMAGES, IMAGES AGAINST WORDS . . . doers, imitators, woodlice, these are our successors . . . they crawl in puddles, in the juice of what is left of 60s—let's light another cigarette, pour ourselves a pint of dark beer, two fingers of whiskey, and lets jack off among the burning images.

A physical and verbal truth that Death TV reveals to us.

The planet is about to explode!!!

We don't have much time left, that's obvious, or isn't, but where are we? We're at the spatial disco, we're in time, we're not in space. Operation *"Solitude It's Always Sunday"* . . . we're here, gelatinous rats, fascinated by tricks and games . . . neon-bodies and impulsions, we're going to decode the sexy message.

We're here, with our words, near the shadow, in bright sunlight, in the wind, with volumes of visible nature, running across green pastures, velvety, facing the intense rage of images.

The seeds are thirsty.

Silence is about to bleed the loving teeth of stardust white. Here, landscapes tell that nothing is easy, everything is pathetic, the whole earth's visible in a body, and that's logical. Robots yell at death, the others do it too, dwarfs and degenerates dream of sailing for Utopia.

Violence, violence, violence . . . hideous young people play with death in the Snow Subway.

Terrifying, I agree, it's terrifying, like that jungle of shanties and suburbs full of steel and trash cans. Girls and boys seek a little bit of warmth, a little bit of love—then militants and moralizers appear, closely followed by evil genies and their poison pens, they rummage through young bodies, and the notion of sin takes the upper hand—bloodthirsty grays open fire on the flock.

A direst experience for the being along with Cowboy Alpha.

Swirls, multicolored streaks, strings of fears and stamping . . . whenever you wish . . . don't hold back . . . don't beg for an orgasm from empty statues—all the signals circle reality—empty transparencies the curtain is torn before your very eyes. Opal with her million eyes reappears in a bone sky.

The Cancer Promenade, Multicolored Death, Death TV, *The Vampire State Building,* NASA's orange-blue views, raw meat cities . . . it was yesterday . . . a trapeze artist on the wire hurries to sabotage the merry-go-round. The planet's menagerie doesn't have much time left.

What have you gotten from dictionaries?

Your name? X, *unadapted idler,* well, it's still better than no one! . . .

Laughing eyes tell you that almost nothing is left.

You're still lacking two magic eyes to illuminate that brilliant speech.

122

It's raining, hailing, nothing is *counter-nature*. Nothing is true. All is permitted. I'm not even up to appreciate this or that. ALL IS TRUE, NOTHING IS PERMITTED—eco-catastrophe (the ecstasy of blue on wild strikes) frost drowns my projects, the fire is spreading—what a great silence today!

I'm sitting in the afternoon's flame, an organ-shaped mouth is qualified as the most somber, a bouquet of twats around the xylophones, fire spreads in the firmament. *A drop of sky in a song . . .*

A SCREEN RIGHT IN THE SKY

The word's hurricane-lamps holds back its tears . . .

Silent figure, bloody wood sighs, all this never ends . . . cries, rasps and tears that we comb, dress like songs composes during the summer, that we make up like refrains carried away on dead waters . . . *"Getting soft Rocking Man, Insurrection Of A Million Minds"*, starched clouds weaving a neon-souvenir, a pink smile in the blue sky, it's really simple . . . the weather is fine . . . the river's waters are clear, period.

A white wave looking like a shadow. I'm not going to complicate something so simple. I enter the Universe shattered. Operation "Here's something To Jog The Molecules, Zip's PUZZLE DEATH, the new porn—the earth has painted her lips, and oranges venture behind the horizon, here, a faded violet, there, an open book—a star dances on a fresh mint geyser, the sky is gloved with hail.

The poet doesn't live in another world. The shadow doesn't speak about its flirtations. I only listen to the void turning, beyond silence . . . flowers scatter their secrets . . . I have no regrets at all. What about you? . . . What a silence in the abyss-margin!

Why are you so sad? (sounds of voices thrown out by reality)—anecdotes are nourished by scrawny cold, dew murmurs—bees follow the path of herbs, and everything that has been said can be expressed differently. Why are you so sad?

Hawthorns want to laugh. On the edge of the path, among the wild roses, naked squirrels dance, silence laps the mauve of the hills. Hokusai and his waves don't know where to go anymore—a crumpled sun, frozen spray on the mirror—snow embroiders on landscape-skin, target clouds dance on black ice.

A hole in the forest, grass forges its beast-thought.

A cigarette in which one hundred flowers swing.

Hawks haven't heard the sky's lace groan—the weather is fine, with his finger in his eye the militant stomps the flowers—I'm not *one* of YOUR compatriots . . . oh! Shit! A guy who invents sentences, and all nature chuckles . . . Yes and no, a show that shouldn't be missed—busting your balls is a trump card in life, all the same . . . a drop of sky in a song, I am a fan of my own fantasies . . . neon flesh growing like virginia-creeper.

Spirals. Inflation. Back-stage discussions. Secret negotiations. Rumors of hot or cold wars. With a closed mouth the light breeze sets fire to the mirror.

I offered a tri-colored Tampax to Miss America with a fire-cracker inside, then the flowers deployed their songs, and all the women in the world shook in the rowboat of my heart . . . brutes, punks, sprites on the chessboard—true silence built those cliffs and rocks, dawn's stones announce the deluge—silvery waves, fire lines in the gumdrop sky, the Universe grinds its teeth, thunder buzzes on the snow. Broken images, engulfed by night, a forerunner sign jostles the hurricane lamp, I close my eyes . . . time is brutally beaten by a blue cigarette . . . Unknown colors in the watershed of light.

Should space remain cold the world will be entirely put to music and into spoken archives.

We spoke for everyone and I tremble as I re-read the journal of my life, the colors warm me, silence spreads, time-slobber—what is happening in my life? In yours? Uh-um in a cloud turned ugly. I've planted thousands of flowers, and all those seeds were buried. Spring spits in the air and deplores its terrible fantasies. The wind has cool hands. Rain jumps over the dunes. Music grows a mountain flower that signs dawn. Blond streets were glassed in by the laughter if bulldozers. A mechanical piano is burning in the moonlight—laughter gets its fill of tears—the day is made endless by a hedge of voices . . .

"Stoned dreams"—a bouquet of sparks sobers the red robin . . . the cat gives up smiling . . . a little dew on the screen. God doesn't have any *luck.* I guess, in the long run, that nothing is easy—sitting idle, the shadow plays among the branches of the Japanese cherry tree—all this excites thinking . . . a cold bomb weeps on the blank page . . . God will be the historian of flowers, and I will be enchanted to become those two drops of water . . . *this doesn't explain that . . .* toasted bread absorbs honey and butter . . . the consumer spits in his own ear—a crescent moon   in the sky, fog plants its thorns on the mauve hills (we've known moments when the situation seemed desperate, and you can be sure of one thing, *this doesn't explain that) . . .*

Chains of words and images unconditioned the word.

Blunders of DEATH TV, and with that form of life the head is first.

THE HORIZON CRACKS. THE SUN SPITS OUT
A WET STAMP.

The sky, barely reddened, opens up with fiery
songs.

Day is breaking.

Blond fields streaked with quick-silver.

A grimace takes the place of TV news.

The sun's mane has nailed a cloud on
imagination. The world breathes. We breathe. A
minute of silence in the wake of images—beautiful
emeralds in the empty alleys—day is breaking, gold
streams onto the lawns . . . *It's hard to trap a moment,
poets know this all too well . . .* the sidewalks of King's
Road blossom, huge neon stars drink the city's tears . . .
bombs, explosions, murders, fights, aggressions, the
Industry of Death tricks life and ventilates great puffs
of hate—robots close their eyes on reality, the four
seasons wear no panties . . . the sky's mouth hits the
white of the eye and devours my comix.

EARTH!!! EXIT FROM DREAMS—(written
crossing fields) . . .

Horizon-pages, 6 am . . .

The weatherman said visibility would be
difficult—rain, wind, and time going by so fast . . . the
wind weeps above the black wheat and floods the
heart-mirror of this morning—the wind invades the
slumber of my cats, and between its fingers it does a
somersault.

Poplars look as if they are taking a walk.

The mist is trying to blur the landscape.

Laughing, tiny details collapse in front of the
flowers.

— A neuro-psychiatrist was running in the

128

grass, etc., etc. . . . an odor has already joined the immensity—and that is where I sat down in the fresh grass. . . .

WRITTEN AND ERASED IN THE FRISCO SKY

A bit of eternity in the pink window.
Blond mountains riddled with poppies and
corn-flowers.

(Stones swallow our tears, a lava flow
transforms the landscape, on its high heels a tidal
wave ravages the West Coast) . . . we chew our cud in
the shade of tall trees, *high on the mesa*, a smell of
burnt toast invades the universe. The stars dance . . .
raisins, nuts, almonds . . . the wind rips the pages of
newspapers and miniskirts . . . perfume and pearls
travel faster than light. Everything quivers in the
Velvet Bay, the Illumination Cobalt Blue Bay—paprika
accompanies the wind, *Cosmic Drag*, Donald Duck
fucks Mona Lisa, the Masked Lobster sodomizes J.
Edgar Hoover—void dances in the margin, sparks rob
the Cold Bank . . . robots impose a violent censorship,
and on the blue screen a beautiful flesh-storm, gusts of
screams and prayers . . . gongs and tambourines,
we're in the blue jungle and we risked all for an orange
girl with a boy's ass. The automatic pilot writes in the
sky *FADED SMOKE*, drifting . . . flood of alcohol . . .
acid hasn't been outlawed yet . . . crazy television sets,
skulls stuffed with multicolored sausages . . . some say
that it's still too early and roll in grayness, the others
arm themselves, to hear and see nothing.

Paradise lost? The fluorescent city's arms roll
on the screen, twisted, broken, they're the streets and
the old films oxidize the young years, flesh cracks as a
sign of mourning.

I'm speaking from very far away from today,

131

and from the depths of the 50s and 60s, upside down, in the middle of undecipherable mutations.

Time opens up in capital letters—the Monkey alibi is solid—sono, stereo, *lightshow*, the video lifelines that we all have within us, like the scream's test-wall that ticker-machines pour into the files. We weren't sure we'd speak about this again, in the sewers of Paris, London, New York, Amsterdam and to repaint both sides of the scenery with juicy, stinking shit undeniably French . . . EXORCISM !!! . . . unnerved bodies groan . . . speed, alcohol, barbiturates, H . . . exorcism to recharge the sweet almonds incrusted in the Blue Kid's body, moving in an old film. Time's crockery dissolves in savage shudders. De/collage of every sound-image. We move very fast in time and space & we write over every landscape in neon.

Anti-death lighting.

Here, bubbles & death, why so fast?

Napalm, Coca-Cola, IBM, ITT, myths, operetta toys, *soap operas*, meditation-chromos, A Festival from Nowhere—the Blue Kid was in Frisco, like a shadow among the guests, like a shadow expelled from sleep . . . a smoke & sound affair, sucker-images that bodies follow like the fireflies in Cherry Valley sky—lives eaten away by minute-metal, clots of death-TV flung at high speed on the Santa Anna Freeway, a few crumbs attacked by pollution.

I see again the old Black woman in Panama City, and Bilgray's Tropico, Panama Rose and Ixca, disorder's bastard asleep, naked on a beach surrounded by tape-recorders.

And Caryl Chessman's insomnia on the

musical chairs of Alcatraz and San Quentin . . . we inhale the odor of human linen and dead salad . . . we know nothing.

A cadaver on the surface of an ocean of beauty spots . . . mutiny . . . a duel on the snow.

Toxic images, prisms prisoners of frost, cement-mixer images, swells like the suns, eye-harvest on the gallows, aurora borealis . . . grass vanishes under the Offset shower, *Tabloid Krishna* . . . the weather was fine between curtains of silence, happy cosmogony in the prompter's box, the old film was blue, the *blue* of a generation on a bandstand, and all that cities have seen and heard in broken syringes and old eye-droppers . . . New York, 1964, the demonic screen . . . several films, *Batman, Flash Gordon, Silver Surfer, Captain Weird* . . . Chinatown, Needle Park, the Bowery . . . Marx ass-fucks the Pope, Dali sucks an old condom that had belonged to Truman . . . and that diligent silent humanity puked into the stable of the American Dream . . . AMPHETAMINE TERROR!!!

Memory's locomotives blow TV antennas.

I saw the cops strip *sick junkies.* I saw *the Gay Scissor Brigades* in the columns of the *San Francisco Chronicle* with the Beat Generation's bastards living in the dawn-weldings, a time for contempt . . .

MOJO NEWS . . . the Spade howled, there were 500 coming from Greenwood, Mississippi to lynch him . . . the Blue Kid cut in the orange of a vision, cut with a blow-torch in the Nerve-sector, outside the scene—blurred dawn, elsewhere with flesh speaking a makeshift slang born of earth-sweat, living colors hanging onto the tender hills of New England, shadow mounts drowned at Fire Island—we were the survivors of that Electric Season.

Uptown, Indigo Off Station, the Snow Subway—everything's blurred, we can't get by anymore, we must push the dirty-finger-curtain aside—A beggar dies on a bench, Avenida Solitario, in black light and stereophonic jolts . . . the shadow barks, screams tumble with the dirty fingers, the antenna-man murmurs *"here, fast, now"* . . . *DREAMSCOPE* . . . with which face should we weep now?

Neon-lianas, red thorns stretched under the skin and the colorless veins of your name rot in the bone-pit of time. In the sleeper's eyes the negative *Quai Aux Fleurs*—damp earth, jumbled, flaccid, black—extra-terrestrial mechanics, a dialogue between heaven and earth . . . continents drifting in mist, salty, asbestos Spring, white sun, disturbing pendulum . . . neon unfurls a tango moon.

The menagerie weeps. Heaps of bones and starfish, tonalities lose their foothold. Nerves yell like cameras. On the branches of laughter gloves consume themselves on the magicians' hands. I've counted the days, the nights, the gaps, the hollows, then blue letters were blurred in the sky's spittoons, with grass bent by fire, and barrels of sores, and wings fluttering . . . Alone on the Heart Strand, I understood that the wind wasn't a ghost. Waves, eddies, signs, clippings, sighs rushing flush with the ground over the Spanish gorse. Target-night, freaky wind, frost bows.

The Golden Gate Bridge wavers, undulates like a plate of spaghetti.

El Paso Motel, Dead Water Valley, don't wonder if I talk to you from so far away . . . I hadn't

134

written a single poem then, speed-funk is indescribable, between spark-fingers the last phosphorescence, slow masturbation in cooling sperm-cisterns. Moving erections, memory-plugged melodies, mopped up by pollution noise that burrows into meat. A tempest of dry ice. *Pinball Machine*, peyote chewed by Nueva Barcelona tape-recorders . . . Indian flowers, snot-nosed peninsulas, a joint opened on incense paper, and flower on a black background, thrown over as the heart wills.

Flower round about midnight, I say you're immortal, I, me, as white as snow, back to the wall, leaning over that bit of skin—so far away, stoned on the back seat of the Buick, in front of that pink villa, in Mexico, contemplating pebble-samples, petrified in that floating bus, from Tijuana to Mexicali . . . round about midnight . . . the shadow of Brocéliande crashed on Acapulco—two very pure notes immobilized over Baja California . . . Methedrine hitting every cell, dirty tickets melting in the smoke, gray things wrecked in the cold dawn, and Flower crucified on the joint-hedge, crazy tomb! . . . the docks, knife slashes, shots . . . musical flushing and entrails placed end to end—Star-gallop in jasper, turquoise and opal stars, *Speedfreak* on the high seas with the time-tatters, with the Peony Kid, in a faint overdosed, blue anemones caught in cocaine crystals, Montana's pink cough, fears, escapes, pains, an orgy of solitudes—we're in the Vomito, crime capitals aren't romantic. We're near the cramp basin, in the arrival of bubbles, wandering from pad to robot-kitchen, from Panama City to New York, FLASH!!! . . . you can say that again! . . . all that was left were my lips around my teeth, and even then!

135

Then the *flash* needle, making my veins blossom once again! . . . I must get out of this, fast, now, and allow music to penetrate the Universe, like the poems drifting in the Bay of San Francisco—silence recorded a little before dawn, the angel tows fog-horns . . . hookers and drag queens motionless on the sidewalks of Turk Street . . . sono penetrating the vague moon . . . sky lit, steamed up shop windows. El Paso, Santa Monica, Sheridan East Corinth, Long Island . . . rain, interplanetary nightclub, neon lights on the nod in the stones of this continent—and all those who fall pushing their bubbles along . . . good God! Eyes are made to hear, and nothing is real enough—so I waited, staring at the corner of a Formica table where a cup of tea was cooling, to make my waiting easier I filled the jukebox with *quarters*, I thought of a face, a shadow hanging onto the vein tree, I soothed the crabs, I held out cash, and pocketed the sachets . . . and SPLAAaasssshhhh! The pain's white capitals were doing the split—and then, one day, just like that, the nervous systems prodigious memory makes a decision, my cells were in a panic, operation *"Let The Shit Go!"* then the metabolic wheel started to spin . . . icy leaks, the great wheels dig into space . . . a light mist made of grimaces, strangling and spasms . . . the sickness marries your body—so, to sleep, sleep, sleep, on my knees begging for a last needle . . . crouched in a corner, shuddering, cramps, covered in sweat—monstrous flowers hit by that white shit, Iron Street, my skin filed by blue cornflowers-puncture-points . . . my eye flat against my ear panics . . . a dizzy fall . . . a horde of red rats attack you, and you wave your arms in the avalanche of cramps . . . and that

136

comatose sleep on a man's back, that wool and cotton space-suit, and guts knotted in alphabetic index of agony.

Grass is scorched. White flowers are turned into blazing serpents. The gates open, you are the first to attend the festival of the quick and dead, you're the switchman of terror. You drive with headlights off, your eyes are unzipped by the ventilators, and meanwhile dharma-skin of the conscience-world is overflowing with blood on the arms of the sun.

We were waiting, bunched together, stinking of sweat and sickness. A guy had just hanged himself in the crapper. The ruins of this sorry feast were frozen hard. Horrible details ambushed under the doormats. I guessed what the headlines would be that pleased the bosses, *Drugs! Big Catch!* . . . you bet! . . . There will be a lot of sick junkies on Frisco's aquatic pinball machines said the *Examiner* . . . a day like any other, cops track down junkies, dealers do their accounts, the CEOs question their computers, and old hookers are moved to tears . . . flakes of recycled crowds, hundreds of meters of intestines will ooze out of Subway halls, great bubbles and spatters, and your veins opened by the dawn semaphore . . . Dawn tells me that from the nerve-drums you must only think of life.

Smack explodes in the hard frost. Blistered images held in puddles. Cops, transvestites, hookers, kids, extinguished in the muffled silence . . . the objective TO BE STONED . . . just high, that's enough, nothing more, dangling implacably, *Junkie Blues*, the bubble fiesta pushed in haste, hauled off shore, a superflash slipping along your veins, time pukes

137

through the organs of pain into the cavern of your neck—the city with the twisted arms, burst veins in the turn, gray dreams rehashed on Long Knives Street, flipping out with the sharp whistles of old photos, crouched in the dawn's locks—that day the sun moved dangerously, lilacs smelled good, the morning star shone, voices within flesh's reach—the Technicolor Kid deported to the forest of dirty fingers, reanimated in the flowery flows of Old Mexico, two green eyes torpedoed, tracer-bullet eyes searching through 1000s of scripts . . . or leaning on a bar, an eye on the high seas, scratching myself furiously, and the Sepia Kid, hair floating between the Buick and the Dodge . . . the mad race of tears in the Mexicali dawn beaten stiff . . . or stumbling on the docks, the autopsy of a slick face in the hourglass of fluid time.

As soon as you try to find a vein, asshole, the copy of your absence drinks from death's bottle.

We didn't die, we're cured.

LSD revealed to us the whole howling, hilarious thirst of body and soul. We drank from that milk in the eyes of a young fairy. Life goes on submerged in modern drugs, *legal ones,* drop by drop, and the voice can no longer be heard, smack-metal-minute, the odor of a distant suicide . . . our society is very oriented towards *drugs . . .* IBM land of the arts, I placed my ragged lips on your back surrounding silence—I am healed, it took time, today I'm hanging out like anybody else—a trip to Nagasaki . . . in his paper-maché sky, the Chinatown angel detaches himself from the old universe blue-fish-eye, pressing on the sexy thermostat, reading the blue journal of absence.

A long silence among so many others took a census of the void, like starving blood, a prisoner of bubbles swallowing colors in one gulp.

Our wing baggage was light.

(I was told that the weather was fine in Mexico City) . . . and in the rearview mirror neon-sprays, an electronic solo in the Hiroshima-Nagasaki glance . . . a blood-flash in electrocuted eyes.

Flower-sob, kid with twisted fingers, smoke and reliefs, blood-filled flowers, a kid in ashes, at the end of night time is sucked again—written in the sky at high tide, faded flowers, faded photos, faded knives, faded stars, a dirty dawn crashes on the city subjugated by screams spat out by syringes, atomized screams vibrating on the skin of time. Curdled blood on photo-rumors, and corner of your broken mouth, so blue—sexy fanfares in the streets of the world, drifting Juicy Fruit Kid, I called this *West Saga Desesperanto*—empty joints, Heartbreak, a rain-death photo in a boy's ass . . . Flower is dead, we'll never know . . . a Thursday, joint-ville . . .

He waited on the pier, near the docks.

Claws tattooing his smile . . . angel or devil? (we'll never know.)

The facts—gun shots, then the body falling in the black water, and no one knew why . . . fair and dark skins . . . rain, he waited.

Chain smoking—in an instant she went out with the *other* guy . . . her body swollen, her face tumefied, she knew, *I love you*—that night she changed beds and assassin.

The acts?

139

Molecules of hate . . . that morning I awake in a hollow, in a dawn of piled high with cramps . . . supersonic turds in the Frisco sky.

(LAST ETERNITY REEL)
ATOMS AND FLOWERS

Smoke pot in your mother's womb! ...
The purity of their wings, the insolence of their youth . . . filter-eyes on the always blank page, and a sensual mauve mouth . . . New York, acts of feeble terrorism and the noise of Import-Export . . . *our revolution's coming of age* . . . the order of the day "an interesting investment, a spot for the fall of France" . . . *school's out forever* . . . the planet is losing weight horribly . . . have you heard about the plot they're talking about the plot of delinquent intellectuals? (dwarfs invent anything at all) . . . *our revolution is coming of age—do you believe in:*

Fresh air, green grass, blue sky, clear & clean water, trees, stars, tribes, crazies, love, peace, electronic democracy, laughter, poetry, freedom?)

If you do it's okay . . .

(To write a little every day and we know that rage only exists on earth. Why co-sign the incidents that don't interest you? A little science-fiction and laser-cameras speak alone) . . . atoms and some flowers, a little fried music announces a dog's life in the aquarium . . . how dawn must suffer! And blue fades . . . I think of Walt Whitman contemplating the great vegetation of intelligence, blessed are those who chat with millions of gods. Children and sailors will own the skin of insomnia.

Me
I want to live one hundred years
— and more
And purr in the grass

All the radios are covered in frost tonight. It's late. Odors of wood fires stroll around. Blond tobacco is on the airwaves. Lamps buried in the sand shine with thousands of fires. Scrawny eyes are bloodshot. From now on we'll be alone, like the gods, always dreaming, in vain, of a universe full of bubbles. Tranquility and silence. Winter's silence wipes what is left of the 60s with a damp cloth. Parking meters of the Universe groan—*Narkophonic Jams . . . Full Tilt Boogie*—waves roll their black wooden eyes, the west wind engulfs the serenity of this beautiful day, I will have to gather all the secrets of next winter.

A HOWL FROM THE SKY IN THE PINK WINDOW.

The neon parade—fire is rising—the planets crack.

Will we escape the violence? (all is possible now) . . . our wounds are healing, they will go around the world again.

Bodies, blue floats.

Soul, air explodes on the track.

Sex, sperm makes a U-turn.

God, in the air time makes a detour.

Blood, I hate meat.

Bone, the Angel has a hard on and comes.

And we're going to get fucked on the way.

SO TO GET AWAY FROM THE BURNS
UNDER A SHOWER OF SPARKS

What is a stranger to the soul and the heart shouldn't be called *vision. As the heart says my days have left to wander.* That isn't the way to settle into solitude.

Pollen, blood, come, sweat, shit, singing our first loves, *we'll all go to heaven . . .* TV antennae dance, death TV sucks every vibration . . . fuck off! Plunge into the universe's groin!—time's circles howl, memory's cavern is a pig sty, God, flamed banana, doesn't look back, He hasn't ordered the massacre of stars—Drunk, stoned, meat loaf . . . flies plant kisses on history's fat bums, we're watching the last western, *evening, morning, thanx again, God speed, Motherfuckers!* . . . a wild soul needs no dictionary, the body doesn't need organization, Western at the Entrance to the Sky, Kali Yug Non-Stop, the pink surf of the jungle strangles neon, last electrified minute ten years later, mauve anemones in my sky . . . highways don't know that the sky and earth meet sometimes . . . children steal a piece of cold wind, shadows aren't crying out tonight. The blind wind and bad omens tie the dream in knots, and the scream of canned currents turns pink.

I sent you flowing to return you to life . . . just look at Nixon, that sexual disaster, the great white feast of our malediction . . . I wouldn't sell a second hand condom to that guy . . . he would have to leap towards something else, for him to get a second soul, flowered and surrounded by colorful butterflies—that kind of silence erases the image of the Industry of Death, the storm of colors bursts the abscess of absolute power—the crowds' gravelly voices pollute your skies and your souls. There is no answer to that . . . huge things begin to live, honed by cold dawn, *no-love* shows its claws, mob-consciences recoil . . . words and songs, filthy dentures straddling thought-vegetables . . . poetry is a rocket, and a free man's laughter crashes on the launching pad . . . next summer's stones will be American, *Nutopia* . . . A vague moon will harpoon lotus-words that angels spit out like clots.

What is the poet's superior logic? The poet is always right, it's written in the sky, and it doesn't matter—the poet is both right and wrong, he likes to do nothing, he takes drugs, if he's an alcoholic, homosexual, criminal, it's a lifestyle, and this eliminates the opinions of one and the other with no bleeding. It's what some very young people understand very quickly, thanks to visual/sound avalanches. They are already high in the sky's dust-covers. But the fact of hitting 40 suddenly, *in the prime of life* imprisons us in the "they say", blood flows, laughs and cries all the way to bedazzlement, and blood has only one goal: PUT AN OBSTACLE IN FRONT OF DEATH AND RETURN YOU TO LIFE.

To go down into the abyss of vision, bothering no one, with the angels, madmen, and children, with the pack of dogs we carry within us—Sing to your heart's content, nebulous panther—echoes write on tattoo-scapes, the sun weeps under the lemon-squeezer, buildings have put on their white dresses and the manhunt is always open.

Fantômas surrounds himself with climbing

furs and dawn resembles a long candle born of a
dream and sorrow.

I say anything at all
a cry in water
"gimme shelter!!"
an electronic raga in the open sky—
a cry in water

Blood repaints that plump, goitrous landscape.
The sky is a wart. Kitchen folklore makes history's bed.
And I, one by one, I pull out language's ass hairs—City
hysteria reaches its paroxysm, let's not talk about the
suburbs'—Operation *"Bad Trip"*. . . We jacked off too
often with that revolution idea, Raw Winter blisters
drag along and a few flake-screams come down to
earth. Circus dogs learn to live in supermarkets . . . sea
foam smothers volcano fires, water flows over words,
like a soft nail file on London on a rainy day . . . The
intrepid traveler and the solitary one can't escape from
the landscapes that we created, nor their violence. The
robots saw nothing. I won't make a wish this evening
. . . Who can dream on the traces of fluid time?
London, a rainy day. Time's tannin tickles the
banks of the Thames, silence is ripped open like a tube
of toothpaste.
Smoke hesitates between two worlds.
The flame-throwers of Total Censorship control
everything, even sexual energy. Censorship causes
the propellers of the marvelous to turn pale . . . the
birthmark of a vision . . . the democratic electronic ear
gives you back the songs of a generation . . . Operation
John Cage, *"Happy New Ears!"*. . . What can we say?

145

Press the button, pull the chain . . . they have changed
my song . . . shit-lit stutters in the prompter's box . . .
Pop-bag misery, today's tube is awful . . . *TV-dinner
knocked, fucked up and zapped in,* I like that . . . Ivy
falls in love with old things, and I go on writing to
various people, I take walks, discretely I'm bored, I
avoid all sorts of people, I hang out, I'm high, I trip, I
travel, I don't make a dime with what I write, others
invent words on time's back.

Operation *"Pepsi"*, *"Beat Your Meat"*, good
and bad news—catastrophes, bombings, genocides—
insects, ghettos, rats, killers, plotters, enzymes, cock-
roaches, all this comes before man . . . Which survival
projects are you talking about? . . . The tickets haven't
been reimbursed, they exploded, and God opens His
eye, ignoring your prayers . . . then the Indians lit great
fires, burning the words that polluted the Great Plains,
the Great Lakes and the shores of the Pacific . . . Words
decimated the Celts, poets and the unstable, but
the great patterns of their laughter will break the
supersonic sounds that hurt the heavens . . .

Windows in flames this morning.

Silence—death makes its bed.

Time's gold is devalued.

The scent of flames listens to what habit says,
and it's midnight, night's bowl is overflowing.

Death must shut up.

The morning operetta seduces cherries covered
with shitty light. It's Spring. Empty forests pivot on
clouds—I know those landscapes very well, they are
brutally invaded by sadness—shadows hang onto
flowers, weighed down by songs.

Jefferson Airplane a long time ago, Nevada,

Colorado . . . a faded pain sleeps in the sands of the West.

THE SEXY MESSAGE BUZZED IN THE TREE OF SILENCE. *Paranoid Blues,* pendulum of explosions.

There's a clock that doesn't chime, an accumulation of errors, an extraordinary push forward. The masses aren't against it anymore, they follow as they shit. The incurable backwardness of words doesn't seem to affect the hopeless revolutionary without a revolution . . . Zippies and Yippies face each other, that was yesterday . . . Psychedelic Fascism considers itself in silence, like a period in history . . . the masses don't understand that parties and ideologies have no reason for being—the rest sheds its skin, every day technological advances solve our problems—false information shakes the Planet, the universe shudders, freckles disappear . . . *Blue Grass*, language can't foresee the variations/mutations, the body doesn't reject the vision that sometimes ignores it at times . . . Chorus of information . . . On the way things change, and yet everything was very clear, to produce, consume, govern, conserve—flesh pivots on reality—music invades the sky where stars are extinguished.

What are we doing on Earth today?

We're doing a lot of jacking off. Flakes and flowers disembark. Sketches frozen in the "they say", the sketch of the drama, of the world.

Time flies and makes you cry.

Pendulum of explosions—blue wounds the shadow—wood enters the fray, unravels the knots of given space, on the way back the signs of the times . . . An axe posted on the heart of the *Punk* Zodiac . . . dice roll on the mirror . . . the other side is closed forever—nights tighten up, the pliers of the wind whine, you can become familiar with God, neon bleeds night—dawn will be . . . banana-shadow.

A streak of abstractions pinches the universe. God is having fun. A bisexual God smokes hash. God takes *a fix*, clasps the blue ropes spouting from the hi-fi channel, bites his nine-string guitar, busts his electric organ . . . then the catastrophes? Wars? . . . soundlessly night opens its wings, a slight tremor . . . the straw man and the man of the street straddled a supersonic turd, patrolling the sky. The survivors don't carry away any image of that world.

Light images are imprisoned in bubbles, the felt pen has become an outlaw. The *media* have manufactured everything. The sexy message buzzes in the silence-tree. The scenery collapsed. The ideological services were overwhelmed. Armed bands looted the supermarkets, attacking passers-by savagely, raping young girls, sodomizing boys, set schools on fire, dynamiting subway entrances at rush hour, hordes of dwarfs were setting the world on fire, millions of Chinese children are born between the pear and the cheese . . . a recapturing of those old harmonies on the screen . . . The Evil Eye weaves the vines of time.

Bureaucracy believes it's time to rectify. A flood of precision. The world, seen from Washington, from Paris, London, Moscow, Peking, is entangled in a complex game of war and peace, negotiations, recycling, absorptions . . . Our Lady of the Snows, an island on the moon and an American flag . . . I won't take back what I have said, nor retrace my steps, nor take back what I have not said . . .

The secret meaning of words lands on the

dunes, escaping from the given or received language. I go through the looking-glass whistling a popular tune.

Drunk, God paints the hills and caresses the forests. Blue speeds, without a license, on the highway. Thousands of youngsters flee the gray suburbs only to land in other places, and I'm going to shit as soon as I can.

There, that's how heaven is destroyed, how flowers are poisoned.

Such tatters have built the world.

Operation *"Reel Fucks Real!"* . . . hell in the city—a tear engulfed in a surplus of signs in a bone sky—the great tear-basin, Fuji-Mojo, Yin Yang-Tidal Wave, flowers, seeds, fruit, wild animals . . . the audition is positive . . . the wind splits in half too, no pun intended . . . the music of West winds rains in my head, look, look at yourselves, look here and there, for an instant, a little inside and there outside, fast, now, God asks you to live in the raw flesh of consciousness. A poet's soul enters childhood without knocking, then it wanders, it can't tune into its birth date, nor in its civil status, nor even to the color of its eyes.

Tonight, near the pond, tenderness overflows. It's already spring. Everything comes from the trees, flowers, odors, the cries of birds, songs, music and dancing—honey drips into milk—the blue of the sky drinks of pure joy.

Can you hear the public complain? Wind-tears say no comment. Anything heard starts to live according to your nerves. That's what creation is all about—shooting stars rain down, smiling—A brain turd takes off. Sunflowers breathe and sing. It's raining.

Mist envelops the hills. The sun is shining. I only have one pack of *Camels* left, a half bottle of gin, two or three *joints*, and God never announces His visit) . . . intervals, zigzags, puzzles, the wind's hoarse voice seems in a hurry to end it all among the dolmens and menhirs, the fresh wind and its throng of nudes enchants us.

All the landscapes dance in my head, like the face-to-face that devours us. Elderberry marrow in the honeyed milk, a sun bubble inhales a shadow. I hope it lasts a long time . . . so, now your slogans? . . . the Universe must dig it! . . . The scream swallows itself . . . blood-orange on a cloud—a rose in the desert, and death, dumb, gaga, hangs out on Earth—blue flashes go bananas and sew up the clouds, and what does it matter whether you're in New York or Frisco, or in London, Kabul or Amsterdam? . . . Electrodes spit, and God sees . . . but will He know what happened on this planet one day?

Blue and orange vapor—a slow shock, soft, deep, liquid, a tingle, a set of geysers, an excess of silence in this quagmire of shadows—God said to me: *Man, I would like to die far away from here* . . . Soprano-dick in the English sky . . . romances, the cosmic *prix-fixe* and a studio-sneeze . . . this book of hours was an amalgam of variations, improvisations, tapes and scraps . . . An island on the moon called Solitude.

It's red, it's blue. Music flows under your feet, an image wiggles its hips—St. Ives, Land's End, Beachy Head, Big Sur, Muir Beach, Mount Bay, Bodega Bay, dispersed beaches and canyons—rocks console each other, images strip in front of the waves.

Operation *"Feed Your Head! Make Your Move!"*—poem! Mercy! Shanti! Satori! Hi-han! That I am? . . . every morning wind-bark cries out, sadness collides with you, and misery—just see the star-studded wrinkles of those who have wept so much, just look at the hamburger-mugs of the *squares* and the militants who have hated too much, look at the average joe, the parvenus, the seedy, look at the lotus murmuring on the lips of those who have loved too much—poets always do several things at once, they dominate speed and slowness, and they are often wrong to *play politics* . . . I hear the song of the poor sufferers, I hear the masses of slaves coughing in the dark . . . Grass takes refuge in the shadow-target. Night shakes itself in front of the TV.

COCA NEON CAMERA SUTRA
FUCK TO THE BONE!

Some time ago I lent a few slogans to the wind, just for laughs. A Yippie fantasy. We were on the West Coast, in our cabins, speeding on the highways in our Buick, Chrysler, Chevrolet, Pontiac, VW, Cadillac, spending our nights in sailor and truck drivers' dives, in transvestite bars and *psychedelic* nightclubs. Some of the men had long hair. Others had short haircuts. Grass was illegal but LSD wasn't forbidden by the rigors of Law—and now that the rain has washed everything, I'm sitting on that fence, I watch the hills shiver—the wind is sitting down playing jacks . . . anything alive shudders with pleasure, like sleeping woods . . . the bubbles of hunger have risked all, and the sky weeps in a hollow. The shadow rises, bleeds a halo. Memory resembles a long flabby lip.

We bump into no-love on all the roads of the world.

Poets have joined together in the center of the mosaic-mandala, electronic and democratic. Old pinball machines are lost in the sky, with the clouds, brand new jukeboxes, and millions of children have died of rage . . . cats continue to play, birds take their veils off, flying hearts don't see the trees weep . . . and writers write, militants militate, video-spheres bleed, newspapers and reviews pile up . . . I don't do anything special, I'm about to leave again, America, Canada, Tangier, Cape Town, I don't know where . . . so, I'm leaving burns in a shower of sparks—it's possible to think that all is well, write poems, have "lovely thoughts", live away from it all, to get really high, talk for the sake of talking, about this or that, in the air . . . in fact, it's true, *all is well*—all's well for me, that's important, all's well for the cats, birds, squirrels, frogs, for sparks, a wood fire never babbles, and cannabis-time flows on the brims of cocks, asses and cunts.

Phony wars, catastrophes, dramas and a thousand miseries, night's bowl is overflowing, meat comes under the knife, silence—a large block of sun hides behind the TV, all the clocks are ventriloquists, and on the volcano of words catherine wheels swallow rainbow colors. Time capsules are bleeding.

(Strong smell of nothing comes from France. Strange, you'd have to leave by leaps and bounds, variable intervals, further away, but towards what?) . . . faded smoke . . . it rises, it relates, and the second soul comes to mind, the zombie is erased, and, of course he returns from time to time, but no longer has any power—slips into the field of vision, the doors of perception revolve, a blue reflection, a flame, a dance, the ball of figure-shapes and souls. They articulate. Enter. Leave. Here-inside and *there-outside.* And God put the brakes on . . . (not so sure, I'm positive of nothing, I've got my eyes open, that's all) . . . in any case *the experience* was beneficial. We are now 1973, it's all over. People have gone away to die very far away, as tourists.

A living world is always dangerous, iniquitous, and no matter where we go we can't escape violence. That's how you travel, that's how you find the sun again, stones, the sky, water, wind, stars, the desert, plants and animals, and that's how we start to live again, and the soul rejoices. This world belongs to us, it is ours . . . like the pioneers of the Wild West you'll just have to recognize each other, contradict each other and communicate, forget certain things, to commit follies by forgetting each other, to dive into the heart of the world and die there . . . tragedy doesn't exist here, but back in the cucumber-world of Social Security . . . For God's sake! They even regret that fire exists! . . . obsessions, miseries, hysteria, we make so much of those things, and no-color shudders with pleasure.

Gelatin, cramps, nausea, the raw being advances in blue dew. Wrinkles on top of the hill. The wind reinvents itself all the time, and we can only express ourselves with words, or with something like that. Everything is inscribed in an air of universal imbecility . . . Poets must be heard now . . . unknown voices must be followed, like you follow a herd of wild horses in the Great Plains. You must live. Everything must live. Now. Forever.

What are they doing? And those? And him? And her? . . . No one knows, just a guess, we pass by, and that's right. All our cells emit, high frequency never varies—from the last telex we learn horrible things—the musicians move, shine, slip, electronic targets, blue and gold unfurl, neon dances, the *lightshow* is within you . . . music for eyes up there on the mountain . . . The evening shadow sets fire to a corpse-laden field . . . The gongs of violence are now quiet—Let's not talk about that ever again, boredom wins—we have to move—a drop of dew falls . . . a tiny sound all in flesh.

A POLAROID RAINBOW

May it all start over . . .

The ruins of an adventurous education of a young man should be prospected. The crazy, vampire youth, so fragile . . . A fixed idea shining under Sally Harmony's scalpel, alias Sally Ka-Ka, a fixed idea that devours an old photo inside my "scrapbook" . . . it's not necessary to invent words to speak about hell. It's clear that those odors escape from crumbling flesh.

The gongs of violence cancel that clog and demolish this galaxy.

Doodling-film of a suffering-language, a poet's ideas polluting the archipelago of silence, stale words rotting in empty streets with phantoms and specters with ridiculous, atrocious, unbearable scenes.

Planets stirred by totalitarian sounds. Explosions . . . banks and hospitals, factories and barracks, universities, penitentiaries, cities and suburbs in ruins . . . A pink moon vacillates and bombards us with sparks. Slobbering throngs escaping from blond suburbs set on fire by stoned thugs, feed on garbage, carrying out strange rites in vacant fields and parking lots. Human sacrifices, ritual killings, black magic, what do I know? . . . hallucinating, tele-manipulated cannibals . . . nightmares ripped from an old film, words torn from robots and technicians overcome by events.

Riot-tattoos, grins, raids, attacks, kidnappings, festivals, police operations, waves of arrests, bloody demonstrations . . . neon has made a date in your dreams . . . shards, ruins, atomized panorama, ossuaries, sounds imitating the odors of rainbows and sprays . . . TV-shards in metallic jungles vomit the bubble-visions of the hanged, strange fruit swinging on the girders of a pylon . . . a powdery night enveloping mercenaries with chromosomes damaged by the drugs that were distributed to them by the Law and Order computer. *The war is over,* what does that mean? The clicks of Polaroid cameras in the backstages of the world. The north wind carries away thousands of objects. Death's laughter is full of smoke. The pest threatens the ghettoes, old hags from the Third World drown in the color film projected by the Red Dykes.

Ecce Homo . . . tragic and burlesque the man kneaded in tears and laughter, blood and shit, that's the way it goes . . . it's only in suffering that man perceives reality . . . *reality?* Did he invent it because of suffering? . . . well, they pissed me off enough, *men* with their arts, with their snide actions, here are some of them in the extraordinary cut/ups, short and tall, fat and thin, crouching in horrible sobs, groaning with joy and pleasure, gobbling like pigs, weeping like whales, polishing their phony prophecies. The women weep also, sneaking away from hiccup to orgasm, they are, of course, obliged to dominate us to save us from any worry . . . anyway, for the moment, men are the ones who make me mad and who piss me off.

"Damn bastards!", that's about all I have to say . . . those shits fuck my head.

May it all start over, bird brains! . . . a young man devouring the prospectuses of this galaxy-film. Empty streets wounded by shards of neon. Ghetto-colors feed your dreams.

A clear fixed idea emerges from the smell of violence.

Stoned hippies in the jungles of the Third World.

"Are you plugged in, fat boor? Well, then serve it up hot, Xerox is in the backstage" . . . you, and your dreams! Shit! . . . a porn panorama jostling the illegible given language . . . Neon scalpel devouring Sally Harmony's sex . . . every message springs from between the thighs of the demonstrators . . . archipelagos of orders rendered stale by reality . . . sounds of pasteurized planets . . . everything explodes! . . . Surreal crowds buzz in vacant lots, stunned in front of the old film engulfed in a flow of garbage, pale tattoos in the eyes of the image-police . . . *the war is over* . . . noises, smoke, cries, cities puke severed fingers and old dentures, nationalist clicks and excrement-smoke clamps, and the wind carries it all away, red plague, the yellow peril and black tide.

"By dint of communicating the guy became an instrument of psychedelic fascism. Kick the flutes of Krishna out, immediately!"

Who is talking like that?

An old photo was nothing but a word,—a loss of memory—gongs and transistors mix their lights of falling darkness. Galaxy-scrawls don't answer anymore . . . empty streets invaded by crazy Blacks . . . a Street of total Renunciation . . . strange rites, unmentionable murders . . . With its complete mass neon ejaculates odor-shards of sexual hunger, vaporizing anxiety on crowd imprisoned in their bubbles. Polaroid Chromosomes don't answer either. Howling hags invade the ghettos.

Bubble-stars announce the end of the world. Neon screams in the empty streets. Sand is buried under your feet. Broken images disappear. The sun spatters us. The wind unsticks the horizon's skin.

Night is torn apart—when you're nowhere reality isn't an empty room— outside branches shuffle the cards, the screams of pollution scorn silence, the last diamonds of conscience decompose under a broken geyser . . . *and this line is the story of THAT death* . . . prisms, rumors, seasons play chess, the elements weave the world's songs . . . we came from heaven (we weren't all born in paradise)—the great North reorganizes light, and on the Seven seas intrepid travelers dance—The story of that death won't abolish the death of others. Life is now merely an illustration, with words on the side of the shade, and in bright sunlight volumes of nature become visible . . . huge green prairies calm the intense rage of images . . . one sign, and you're in all of reality, far from the dangerous semantic traps . . . that's the way it goes, a "trip". A flower that opens, a blue flame, and it's all over. What the shadow leaves behind blurs our trajectories.

A smile, a grimace beheads the clouds.

Two blackbirds go through a curtain of rain and vanish among the red pines.

Realities full of charms. The wrinkle-lipped mornings that we have experienced in the merest detail. Daylight. The gears of the daily grind weep in front of the unclimbable walls of thorns and nettles. The wind strips time's tune.

An event, a violet spot was dyed blond—flowers' prisms howling to break eardrums with the trees only to say they have no secrets—solitude buzzes . . . a Western at the gates of heaven.

Emeralds and wild bushes asleep on the granite.

Here's a syringe full of tears, and there, grass shivers.

Chance sinks straight down. Dew lands on our lips like the sound of a bonfire. Chance lisps, it's ass between two chairs . . . as soon as chance stops lisping, grass turns green . . . the universe is partying, and the dogs run with the wolves in their eyes . . . blue icicles on the Heart Reef . . . London beheads silver echoes, and the city, anchored in eternity, begs for a little sand from metronomes and murmurs. Noise is noise. Dawn coughs between the walls of silence. Fire spits on Big Ben's huge balls . . . gently night folds over the highway.

London in a dawn-cartridge, in the broken void, leading the wind—this morning the planet/garden was all red, continent-scheme where the wisdom teeth of a generation rot in slow motion—silently frost empties the pond. Pink eucalyptus trees are dying. An immense lack of communication fills the planet, silence unmakes the river bed.

Silence and famine riding a cloud. Landscapes full of tears. Fury and blood from one end of the world to the other. Excrement-language around wrecked men. Toboggan-vision, rot. Animals having no country, a society with neither males nor females. (We can do without anything, from the first page to the last—my goal isn't to judge the propositions of one and the other, nor on what to drink or eat, nor on the46 chromosomes of urban guerilla warfare, nor . . .) —embryos wiggling in the pale winter sun—stars, comets and satellites beyond the broken lines of the horizon, genetic information for all . . . casually, a computer explodes in the suburbs of Technopolis . . .

An indifferent face, gray and ageless, having the normal number of chromosomes, a face begins spontaneous division, *cut/up* which sells life and death to X and Y and Z chromosomes . . . heterosexual face, girl and boy scale, a contrary face doesn't have the right to enter, girl-face doesn't have the right to leave . . . a redemptive face receives grass as a sacrament . . . a wave of mud to bless the lineage on its way, muddles by the numerous mutations.

Saving genetic combinations. Don't play the apprentice sorcerer too often . . . Crazy Blacks dandified come out of the walls with the cockroaches—extremely putrid odors escape from the ghettoes, footballs and starving rats are released—Blacks chewing cigarette stubs wait for dark nights with crapper-Chinks, neurotic Poles and recycled chimpanzees . . . crazy Blacks will blow up more than one *stetson* when we will have finished shooting the last ecological Western.

Ecoshit, of money and arms . . . and Mr. Soul straddling the President, big prick Blacks that we displace with their empty eyes on the Jewish screen in the Bronx . . . TNT brays for the poor Blacks with

163

napalm and gelatin, the usual procedure of the meat industry, raising decibels, and over there, a bit of gray cloth dripping with grease over Spanish Harlem— we're there, with our whole words and our cut words, we're there and we eat our own shit, we're the emulsion of shit-words.

A camera visa for another time.

Who do you think you are?

Some catatonic hippies demonstrate . . . a voice: "Your sleeping bags stink! Your hair stinks! And your feet! Your asses! Your cocks! You all stink, bidet scrapings! Crypt-jerks! Pinkos! . . . You're entering the Fork-Era, you're on the Manson-Nixon Pox line, you're the Digestive Carnival" . . . screams, jostling . . . I was the Bilgray's Tropico ventriloquist, mind-vision, bones and soul, but the old hippies still want to choose their words. Summer will be hot for the losers.

I am the pulpy scenery. I am a *pin up* and the slamming door. I am you. I am myself. I am that English village sobbing over Miami Beach. I am sitting in the bar, near the nightclub, close to the golf links in Carmel Highlands. I am Malibu Beach. I am Key Largo, Key West. I am that street riot. I am those carbonated tears. I am that *showbiz* embryo. I am that TV screen and that Comix. I am the record of your own life. Watch out, tadpoles! The Brain Police are everywhere, recruiting its agents in industrial jungles, the underworld, middle class and sexual proletariat. I think that the time has come to cut your hair and to change your uniforms. Horrible, provocative things babble in the dead cities. Filthy colors sparkle through the psychedelic penal-years. There are no more poets. They're all dead. They continue to speak on the scratched record of happiness merchants . . . broken lights cruise behind the shacks where hamburgers are sold . . . masses of

obscene noises on the ideological merry-go-round . . .
you're forewarned, you absurd idiotic jerks . . . bloody
kapok spatter morgue sounds.

You're forewarned, don't grease the paw of a
one-armed man, because I'm here and I can do without
the first page. Embryo-comet breaking down the face
of XY of the crazy Black . . . Landless animals wiggling
with embryos in food and drink beyond the pale . . .
Info possesses you, spontaneous division forces you to
come and go . . . cigarette stub chewing Blacks vanish
in the *Soul* Western—Braille TV has produced an
excellent afternoon—We devour the sky, and decibels
provoke the dead cities using our camera visas at the
very first page . . . cut/up chromosomes and colors
cruise in the pale winter sun.

I sell life and death, girls and boys. I am the
cosmic dealer. Along the road you'll find your own
skulls devoured by apprentice rats and the crazy Blacks
will eat your white livers . . . Blacks that explode before
the end of the shooting of the film . . . empty arms and
eyes, gray industries, guerilla-words . . . Do you hear?
Can you hear them? . . . ventriloquists' souls plugged
into digestive devices of operetta Chinks.

I'm hot pressure-decor. I'm carbonized sobs.
I'm that seedy nightclub, *Bork Tropico.* I am the right
to enter and leave. I am that wall. I'm full darkness and
dawn. We're all here. Everyone and everything. With
our shitty visions and the way we compose words.
Rotten sleeping bags above Miami. A Swami-morgue
bulls hitting in the subway. I'm that street riot, cutting
your own lives and jamming your brain waves.

Nixon and Manson are profiled on that wall.
Pink flash imitates their movements.

Neutral words twinkling in the streets of London.
Cut/up scream over Key West.

I am the automatic gate.

Famine-silence at the end of night, a spectral pinball machine swallowing the tears of a generation of stutterers—night falls, *flop!!* . . . a little white magic to calm sexual hunger of the working class . . . crazy Blacks jack off furiously in the back stage of the Crazy Horse Saloon . . . sexual mosaic ads—*where are we?* as the pages go we become stale. The visible mutation of the message delivered by the grimace merchant.

Planet Earth doesn't answer anymore . . . silence cracks . . . voices burst behind the clouds.

A sign of life carried away by a voice in tears.

We're finally leaving dreams and the infinity of cheap junk—we're always with the times, *we're not in space*—we're here, beaten down by political fiction, and the flowers smile as soon as night loses its footing, then they go away, from void to void, with bent heads.

THE ASTRONAUTS HAVE RETURNED

The astronauts have returned. Psychedelic babies have reached maturity.

The Soviet cosmonauts said:

"We were expecting you. And we were waiting to see what the others had already seen before us. Of course, we've read a lot, and, naturally we imagined something, uh, um, well, it turned out differently . . ."

Outside the space ship the cosmos looks like an abyss, a bottomless well. The earth looks flat, and it was only by looking at the horizon that we could see its spherical shape.

Black cosmic night. Raw stars. Sun—a red disc embedded deep in the blue-black velvet of eternity—remarkable acoustics.

The cosmonaut remaining in the cabin can hear the sound of boots and hands of the one walking in space against the sides of the spaceship.

From the Earth you can't imagine anything like it.

Under this black surface they expected to see *something* rigid in stones, outside the ship, listening to all the worlds. Music with nothing and by no one. and the Earth lost in blueness.

Sounds, *flashes*, *eco-horizons'* bony holiday air, and cosmic stars on a raw gold background.

Seen from the cosmos a twilight eye of black velvet. Fascination. Hallucination. Without false simulation, you can't imagine anything comparable, and on the radar screen I stared at the order coming from below: *RIGHT HERE, WRITE NOW* . . . all worlds are audible . . . Orange caressed the blue coast, abandoned on the seat of dreams . . . no real danger, only the exaggerated curve of the eco-horizon.

A camera stabbed by an earthling.
White's glove slaps the red disc.
Cosmic insolation for the Soviets.

Sky music, air waves, shadow-graphs, murmurs sown by the angels of earth. Landscapes, traces, spots, sounds, and void welded to human movements. We enter. We leave. We're inside. We're outside. *Electric Rainbow, Space Agency Bulletin.*

I oscillate inside someone else's words. Lost, reckless, in a bowl of screams. A little pre-raphaelic fear. A Russo-American cut, and several years between three experiences.

An after-glow pierces dawn. A current of water slow and heavy. Thick, mossy, stringy, gummy things . . . a counter-sky belonging to that old Western, American colors . . . San Francisco . . . scars burned alive by a laser beam.

Our baggage of wings was light, and I was told the sun shines in Mexico City . . . I know that the world continues to be wrong, and that the dead ventriloquist hands claim that Nature looks poorly. What's left of Nature today?

Nerves hesitate. Hearts don't beat anymore. Ink sticks in your throat. Neon-scissors drown.

A tear in what's left of blood—huge sobs tinkling like cherries, as if to say *adios,* as if to tell you *adieu* with its eyes in Indian summer milk—as if to say that the belly-furrows ought to be named after flowers and fruits.

I regroup the pages of this journal that stirs ten light-years.

A second-nature coma, and ashes squeak between my teeth . . . reality breaks into dream-folds . . . so, just think of the huge insignificance of a book . . . Fuck it all, trash-memories, nervous breakdowns . . .

the eye's locket bursts! . . . you find yourself high as a kite, and you don't know why . . . you don't know why you're healed, you came a long way, that's all. At times we feel that we're terrible assassins.

The cold crowd lacerates the sky behind the real world. And me, breathing here at 13,000 meters up with that fruit swollen with milk, born in the heart of a star . . . absent-mindedly *junkies* are spewed back by time's test-tubes . . . a shadow equinox . . . "with that mummy submitted totally to the image,", Shiva, Kali Ma, Jesus Superstar, etc. . . . full mouths stick up a sign . . . there's time to tiptoe out.

Tea blooms in springtime battles . . . like drugs . . . that's the way pot vanishes, and the black lysergic revelation . . . old brain-transfers you're forewarned —tear-covers and faded bellflowers, dawn, dawn-recipient—the tears of a generation evacuate the cool child . . . they all wept, even the astronauts wept . . . everything evaporates, even the conscience/world in the image-sound jungle . . . postal dust, synchronized visions, and a fire-tattooed Atlantic mixes its voice with the sands of the Gobi desert, silence escapes, survival lines are visible.

The cameras scan the cosmic void.

Our ocean-planet is blue. We're tuned into the worlds. Stars on a black background, antennae erected at twilight.

The shadow defrocks proverbs and scream bindings.

Defunct April stabs the rain.

Black and Jewish skins on display.

American colors. November, Kennedy is assassinated. Owsley makes LSD for humanity's greatest good. *Right here, write now.* Snoopy flipped out, the lotus-eater doesn't answer anymore . . .

169

(Paris-Match, *June 30ᵗʰ 1973, "Skylab: 28 days in the beyond", an Article by Raymond Cartier.* THE ASTRONAUTS HAVE RETURNED.)

At the speed of light this is my version that is torn in flight. We were really forced to act that way, six hundred Japanese hoped so . . . international salt-shakers in the cabin of the burst satellite . . . American nerves wakening the base-sounds, adventurers gravitating around fields of stars. The three photo-men seemed to be asleep. Toilets and word lists, the destinies of electronic champions, camera-shears from Missouri.

Doctor Montezuma's Hymn to the Ventilator . . . you'll know the universe and the gods . . . French cleaning ladies in suspension, bathing in pots of cold cream . . . indispensable for a few days, heightening their voices, sucking cosmic rays.

Vacuums climbing ultraviolet urban zones. Sky 73 in the harmony of spheres, forming a whole, Conrad, Kirwin, Weitz . . . an experimental menagerie, tainted objects, demolition on earth—Captain Sun is responsible for food and water—will soon be dead, vaporizing euthanasia Texas, with no help from weight, congealed, like Lexington in vinegar . . . wants to know if the hallucinating traveler of no return has something to say—guinea pigs determining the weight of their organs, circumstantial sketches, spatial information . . . the astronauts inventory the final phases . . . Phase 1: recognizing space, degree zero, quite formless—avid crews, embrace the whole thing.

Do you remember? Three Russians, a mechanical technical accident, or? . . . 433 kilometers of distress . . . Houston Stormfury at the time of catastrophes, the fall of old dreams in a urine analysis. Three centimeters of Skylab, *Hurricane NATO* . . . the

170

eye searches the earth, sometimes reaching ecology . . . an intensely visible planet.

The Geography of the Universe, phase 2: a permanent acquisition for humanity . . . 29 anomalies to combat every year . . . snow and rain men . . . the sun pumping excrements in fusion . . . future men will be the masters of the energy of matter . . . an avalanche of time—ears volatilized by experience, America's distress turned into stars—ocean-cubes in the atmosphere, order abolished in the true Cosmos . . . *the astronauts have returned* . . . bip-bip of the old dream . . . incredible visions, two and a half billion dollars saved *in extremis* by Sweet Missouri... an ultraviolet rainbow, operation *"Cold Cream"*—the astronauts were pieces of bread, Karwin and Weitz transparent, eating with straws, dollars floating in fields of stars—a cosmos with no language doesn't know itself yet . . . who knows who will be energy?

Skylab adventurers are intrepid travelers. Astronaut-bases, wide awake men, interchangeable photos, mental space cameras sucking ultraviolet voices . . . recognizing the three dead Russians in Stormfury . . . probe-crews . . . grapefruits made in space, out of cut/ups, turn in flight, gravitating into Missouri's ultraviolet rainbow . . . will die because of those circumstances—leisure of the future—Phase *Orange* a focal conscience-catastrophe—Zone doesn't answer anymore—swirls of excrement, distress-energy . . . the NASA eye searches America turned into a true cosmos . . . bip bip bip bip . . . ultraviolet toothpaste quite hallucinatory . . . 600 Japanese cutting American nerves in Houston . . . the call of the sky . . . the future will teach us. *The astronauts have returned.*

171

AMERICAN COLORS

At that very moment American colors and Soviet colors were in space . . .

The suburb eyes of Los Angeles mixed with vertigoes, to mobs of posters and billboards, to flashing signs, pushing sexes to the end of their ropes. The great sexual hunger landed on the Oakland Ghetto, crouching under the Bay Bridge . . . A zoo of bitterness, poverty, hate, violence and idiocy . . . a narrow world where tenderness survives even though eroded by the spiral of the system.

Voodoo night—the dead dance on the city of twisted arms—Old movie and burlesque tickets carried away by the wind. A Californian leper-colony . . . televised mirages, taxi-shards, a sexual heat wave . . . I see them all in a flashback on the luminous posters, in sexy cotton balls, in the inventory of dead skins.

A few trips . . . El Paso, Santa Monica, Frisco, Seattle, Vancouver . . . tears as blue as the wild iris of Big Sur . . . Pulverized images inside the show, or in a song I had heard at *the El Panama Hotel . . .* personal screams and messages, and the light songs of Police alarms . . . a tailspin into nerve-mold—words scattered under a microscope . . . Times Square, the Strip, Avenues B & C, blueprints of Grant Avenue—I think it's time to talk about the astronaut's mental equilibrium, brutally mutated in an unknown milieu . . . what bothers us, *what does a man feel like at more than 28,000 feet up? . . .* and what to think about the extraordinary reticence of Leonov and White exactly when they put their spatial cells on?

Was a question of the natural grayness of the man who, body and soul, were participating in a fabulous world premiere?

What to think of the converted and of those who became unhooked?

According to White McDivitt he felt a kind of drunkenness . . . A distant voice, endlessly repeats, WAR IS A HUMAN THING, WAR IS A HUMAN THING . . . sprays of neon light on the windshield, an electronic solo in the gazes of Hiroshima- Nagasaki . . . the spurt of blood in the electrocuted eyes begging for a meager orgasm . . . painful fragments, emotion retires from the poster.

PENETRATE THIS WORLD BEYOND WORDS—

ACTION—death in a corolla is ambushed on the corner of a street . . . brief sequences . . . nothing would have happened if . . . heavens streaked with black bile . . . Panama Rose said: *We have no time to waste with these gentlemen* . . . Joe Verminex was ordered to watch over them from afar, from a suburb of frozen fingers occupied by the sexual proletariat.

They came back, alleluia! . . .

"God is absent", said one of them.

"Hang up, Rosenberg! You horny viper!" . . . answered the other one.

A fantasy that others had imagined tuned into all the worlds . . . someone came to buy back His Father's Kingdom—bright circles grasp Leonov's hands, who then leaves his seat at the wrong moment, outside the cabin he's dazzled, as if someone next to him was welding—Lightly, Leonov presses his hands on the side of the ship that moves exactly the way he does, but in the opposite direction . . . of course, he swears in Russian . . . swearing in this extraordinary moment . . . that all the clowns of the Supreme Soviet State are

174

cocksuckers, that the comrades are starting to piss him off . . . and Belaiev heard it all.

There were a few difficulties for Leonev, (a few worries), when he wanted to return to his spaceship. And he knew how impatient the people on earth were waiting for the end of the experiment. He must have moved a lot in a very short time, with the merest push the space-ship moved away from him, and the KGB bastards, the red spooks got closer.

Leonov and Belaiev saw the *red stars,* they didn't see God. McDivitt and White saw *the stars on the American flag.*

Leonov watched the somber side of the sky through the rays of the sun, pale, very pale—it seemed as if someone had sown black and gold stars—the lenses of the cameras heard it all, the Houston ear sees everything . . . the immense opacity blushes . . . in the cabin you had to do everything, you had to come in and go out, go out and in.

You'll wait forever in the brightness of that light.

Watch out, words die at the slightest pressure . . .

Leonov leaves his seat and watches the dark side of someone who is welding. How pale he was! . . . The sides of the spaceship are attacked by pieces of stars.

Scanning the emptiness of the cosmos (that well of hardships) lost in the luminescence, against the clock, returning to the blue-orange, at the appointed time . . . on earth the CIA and the KGB carved time into propaganda units . . . brief precise orders . . . the punks become lyrical . . . against the sky B & L wiped their hands on a sunbeam—others had already seen that, *while speaking to God* a long time ago—the cosmonaut's very slow movements felt the   alienation, and yet they heard the spaceship . . . no mention, in their reports of the sexual hunger in space . . . once again, the sky glimpsed through the rays of the sun.

American colors—someone sowed stars . . . they heard voices . . . the laborers of space didn't see the stars scattered by the CIA and the KGB—the cameras came, red phosphorescent orgasms outside the ship, and the earth scratched by blue . . . *coming and going* . . . Seen from the cosmos the black and blue velvet leaves the air's seat—emitting from mouth to mouth, that the welder hears on the sly—can you imagine anything deader and sadder than a flag? . . . luminous signals disintegrate the jukebox . . . Space Opera . . . the uninterrupted enjoyment of the camera registering future emptiness.

Chunks of stars, solar oranges . . .

WORD ECHO

Who dies on that road, in a black Cadillac, repeating *I want to pick it up . . . ?*
A legend threading its way with colorless blood through the walls of the city.
Violence. Mystery.
Died on the road, on that little dirt path, *Cielo Drive,* in the middle of boreal trash, facing the assemblage-horizon of an uncertain decade, searing, desperate, breaking silences and words.
It's early. I must shave, take a shower, dress, have lunch. The first televised news lands in the bathroom, a distant suicide makes me shudder . . . daylight weaves a veil of blood around the buildings —a blurred film breathes in the empty margin— nothing has changed, operation *"For Who Wishes To Hear . . .* 'So, let's wake up abandoning another piece of life, I ask myself "what makes them write?"
There have been many festivals, the one of Pure Idiocy, the one of Spitefulness, there were huge gatherings, Celebrating Promiscuity, Word Echo Solstice . . . let's put aside phrases and historic words, agents, spies, terrorists, agitators, hitmen and extra-terrestrials . . . dreaming I was cut in tatters of immaturity and limit, and my multiple lives were reduced to zero by destiny . . . they carved my tele-mechanical sex when I decided to write, then I crashed into the wall of Beat and Hip stupidity . . . so then I left, flashy in someone else's clothes, avoiding the polluted air-capsules of *revolutionary* figures—I was the man with the short hair, the man in the gray flannel suit—The Standard of Being Stoned worked day and night (and I never could connect and soar with them) in spite of the insistence

of the Psychedelic Fascist Agency . . . Yesterday's
dream of today in the frayed afternoon . . . a bomb in
the crapper at the Guys & Dolls a week later . . . the
Cosmo fiendish Agency against the Drugstore of
Heaven . . . strange automobile accidents, defamatory
murmurs, curious overdoses, sinister communes and
permanent harassment . . . I left, and when I spy them
in the windshield I feel sick . . . I was the target, I still
am, even though all my books have been published
. . . Trinket Brigade, Amulets and Dirty Fingernails
collapse on the pile of rags of this decade.

Historic festivals in the windowless sink.

My lives decided to write themselves in the
time capsules I've been collecting for such a long time.

Who dies through those walls in middle of
psychedelic trash? Who died so uncertain while he
was shaving, thunder-struck by the fool conforming to
the rules' feeble message?

A suicide's first televised journal and the word that escapes you. Pure idiocy and public mores in the fuzzy clothes encircling the edge of an electrified minute, between Honolulu and San Francisco—in a dream reduced with the collapsed figures of operation *"Day And Night"*—dirty nails murmuring to the second *underground* skin . . . the *junkies* of the 50s and 60s had fallen asleep on the already written pages, a shower of cold and burning points breathing close to my body. A blurred film faced the silence and brouhaha of people coming into the city— unexplainable , distant spitefulness . . . let us leave aside the words, the narks, the followers, the ragged men, the losers—someone else avoiding what makes them write on the walls of the city . . . I was the man in the gray flannel suit, the Ragged Agency beat sex to death under pretext of *liberty,* and God knows what colorless liberation . . . died on the road, dead, the victim of an overdose, dead under the influence of LSD . . . I dress, a veil of blood masks the top of the mountain, the Amphetamine Cowboy lunches in the bathroom, the enemy is ambushed in the empty margin, protected by sono and a purple fog of incense and cooking oil—in the distance a black Cadillac, and a gathering of horizon-consciences.

THE ZIM ZUM LANDSCAPE

A felled tree reinvents time—a dirty song in the depths of time—amphetamines have eroded night, we will no longer be alone in this tidal wave of streets, poplars sing, maple trees and hickories nail dew on this mandala, I run after the fog, the fog that offers itself to anybody at all, just like that, without knowing why . . . I remember those fights with the strands of night over the Golden Gate Bridge. . . .

Blue, solitude buzzes (green eyes in evening gowns, dreaming, blinking), chance-blue in the center of the brain-failure. We're on the freeway, PACKING UP & GOODBYES, the ruts of the brain feel great love sorrows . . . a harvest of sparks, just listen to the wind—wood screams on the corner of a shadow—rain and cold have created this calendar, and on the other side of present time space and the little stars that light up in the evening, a Western at the gates of heaven, Cannabis Junction, Snowhill, Primrose Hill, noise rotates infinity—the jaws of dawn on every airwave—radars, sonars, jumbo jets, tragic effusions, crumpled porcelain in present time's den bristling with evil *dibbuks* . . . rain begets camouflage that mercilessly betrays the daily grind . . . colics and coughing fits bring us together . . . those whose hearts are too petty ruminate like emaciated cows—Liberty, white mint, our gazes turn into icicles, those who feel like captives of dreams have no wings, and hear neither one or the other—puns are superimposed indefinitely, prodded by cloud-images . . . cold colors, sad songs, death visits museums, new flowers pack up jigsaw puzzles and the rain's punches spare no one.

181

Water-carrying colors, heavy night nets, silence breaks you apart—cold colors in the rain know that death isn't favored by nature, and water disguised as tears shouldn't be mentioned—on an emerald line silence protects pale flowers that twist around the window.

Noise bothers infinity.

Flash-rose sighing under a scarf of fog.

Broken air turns around the airport.

They claim that the situation is complicated, Zim Zum landscape opens up onto a few reflections . . .

Clouds, traces of salt, a scavenger-sun, alphabets of broken fingers, childhood's embers die like weeds—a nonchalant eye, a tongue lashing, a string of dreams, a bushy void . . . all that rules in any kind of wind, until the next shower . . . colors weren't hungry behind the clouds.

Horizon-bubbles that my tears swallow, black waves and clamors gag herbs . . . the sky is decomposing (we felt a tenderness for all things you can't even imagine) . . . a pyre-twilight caresses time's fur . . . fruit twisted by foam, the hurricane addresses the tides.

A Polaroid rainbow, a prayer full of claws—I bleed noise to feed silence—I'm from everywhere, I'm from nowhere . . . flakes of stones and jigsaw puzzles . . . sobs . . . you might say they holler like the deaf, like eyes inhabited by silence, like the wind carried away by a stream of poisoned saliva.

Corny brains advance slowly and quietly.

Time-table—souls creak—the rest sink into the sewers of gossip . . . I shit on the balcony of the Consulate, billboards were on fire, and water came from God's mouth . . . *Kentucky Fried Chicken, Pepsi*

Cola, Blue Movie, Players, etc . . . hamburgers bury their dead . . . *THC a safari every day,* Neon Park, Zazen Alley . . . a song, "You're filthy. But You're Handsome" . . . colors have adopted all the flowers, good humor dives into vermillion, and tongues are unwound under a steel sky.

If God regrets nothing, I don't either—Sad dead people won't go far and neither will you—the sun has puked a billion snakes, fire has harvested the jukeboxes, scissors salivate, and you have a hard time keeping up with me . . . the cosmonauts' empty uniforms leak weights and measures, seaweed applauds sand that refuses to question the stars—the horror-circle closed by the Evil Eye—cosmic signals, publicity gestures, scarlet battery lights up the window . . . I dance with X-rays, cold scissors salivate, hate babbles . . . let's tear the veil . . . the soft typewriter delivers us to mirages and falls asleep in dust. Robots have ambushed themselves in the *DOPE* fuse . . . grass isn't only washed in laughter and tears . . . empty mirrors announce the Spring . . . prisoners of flowers, and on the other bank the clouds jostle each other.

AN ISLAND ON THE MOON

When we're in hollows shadows tie knots with our dreams on sale and our drifting wandering in vacant lots that encircle the technological ossuary, on the way we smile at the flowers jotting everything down, day and night we're in the domain of songs —displays of meat bleed, frozen foods rot, supermarkets are battle fields like illegible landscapes. Crumpled by speed—*stoned*, confusing the colors, I write while I chew on cedillas, and I lose myself in the fog, recreating stolen time . . . well-named unbreakable stars—*an island on the moon—Mary Jane sez Happy Xmas,* and the weeping flowers follow the wind. They point at you, like blood shed that straddles our words. We're the masters of waves off shore . . . obscure stitches on the launching pad of laughter . . . a rusty tear in the hollow of the vision-wave . . . we come as we scratch, we repopulate mirrors, snow dazzles us . . . midnight already, noon already, then frost loses its foothold and babbles, tremors on the window sill—a target that is all of space . . .

The sky's spare parts are off on a honeymoon. Prophecies pour out of the jukebox. We're inside the almond-night . . . could you be insolent enough to believe the miraculous tricks and lies of the governments of the earth? . . . one day the Ocean will slit clouds' throats.

We may have dazzled a generation, and blue tea erases the deletions that yawn in front of the computers of the Brain Police. Robots plunge their fingers in your mouths, the shadow only dreams of azure, never of people. . . .

185

Hollywood Burbank Airport, flowers dance on the windshield . . . words squashed in my pockets will land in the ears of the deaf . . . transmission of thoughts in the back seat of a Buick . . . (what's the answer? . . . The question is a crystal ball, a postage stamp drifting around the Ocean-Planet . . . who wants to walk on clouds?)—mauve brunettes, blondes draw in the sky—I see the *call* of seagull incrusted in a cloud . . . Naked, stars swallow light, and flowers bounce on the ruins of tranquility . . . Old stones dream on the Great Plains and nothing happens, the wind's propellers lie down.

Shadows, gusts of wind, rain, blue cigarettes, gray stones crushing the field of vision—heart-world *Yi King*—images in love with all the windy words, every sign explodes . . . every electrified minute poses the same question . . . and thought wounded by Death TV pulls out the hairs of a cloud . . . Nothing happens. Sometimes childhood catches you in the throat like a wave . . . a tide of tears . . . Watered tomorrow.

Dreams for sale, silence within my eyesight. Our secret gardens fight against the density of winter's raw vibrations, made known to you by the shadow's torrential neon lights. With a single look discovering the ocean and its foliage, the naked soul, dolmens discovering the silence when the river carries a pyre of bubbles away . . . we're here, with our words, libido-typo and a sexy diver's suit . . . amphetamines bite into night, phosphorescent clouds . . . and hail strides across the plains . . . from rain to rain perfumes feel our faces—robots' cruel tools set fire to this day's end grasped by rain—a white stone lies down on a record, grass peeks out of the snow hitting you in the back.

Stoned in the woods . . . deep inspiration among the branches of eating and drinking, laughing and weeping . . . standing I interpret a point of the dawn (vertigo has no ulterior motives) foam soiled by snow mourns this mandala.

Sounds in snow-water—*Polaroid Blues*—the sound of shattered glass tells us that emptiness is ageless—with great speed the sun rises in the sky, and with all its weight the wrinkle-impulse turns the bone-lock of violence and paranoia . . . hate and political hallucinations blacken dawn . . . dream-waves within reach, naive souls yield to neon, and once more silence caresses a taxi-cloud as soon as words fall from your lips. Bewitching void music enters everybody, A RAINBOW FOREVER—crumpled seasons, cold chasms—idiotic mouths forcing flowers to fade—we're inside our bubbles and green wood dries before images do. *Naked & stoned in the woods* . . . kilometers of noises . . . songs live in the streets.

SPAGHETTI JUNCTION

Multicolored smiles on the road. Spaghetti Junction . . .

A few tears broke against the hedge of lilac trees, with sly images, snow-drops, primroses and violets . . . many-colored waves in the pale sun gained a little time . . . a secret smoke in which I drown . . . rumors, I hear mouths blossom, their fangs in the humid moss—ambushed in a bottle of *after-shave* a dead man crushes his bones, neon cracks—*Nuclear Fuck Bits & Pieces*—who is in those empty streets with jets of echoes and ultraviolet ricochets? Who? Death's disturbed singing strips flowers and petrified souls . . . rain doesn't speak that language, nor dead birds abandoned in empty streets . . . the bizarre creations of silence, seeds gloved with pearls, crowds germinating in dew . . . I only have a few wrinkles around my eyes, they're disappearing in smoke . . . God hatches a dildo on the ashes . . . and a few days ago I jotted down: *and that's the ultimate on drumming, Lee Crabtree . . .* three days earlier A.G. told me he had committed suicide . . . death always wants to tell us something—images tremble, robots hand out the roles you must *play*—inflatable instructions of the assassins of nature who invented the word HYGIENE.

Some voices murmur on history's table. The game consists of sublimating the last squawk, and the wheel's music, well, I think it is better to steal the Grand Lama's oranges than to be a street lamp in Belfast or the idol of youth . . . and mirror playing (Surrealistic procedures and old lace) of beings who feel like dissolving souls . . . I find myself in the middle of a red stain—Technology's fanfares will never replace interdiction to create, to enjoy, to live, and the social filth of everyday life has made that flabby music that everyone has in his eyes—silhouettes strangled by rain . . . the last letters of our alphabets plant their laughter in caramel-images. Anyway, I shone without the help of your fucking sun, the sandman wanted to sell me the shadow that was overpowering him . . . today the sun is laughing inside an ink spot.

Sleeping Blue Note—heads ripen between heaven and earth—transistor-sexes parade on the outer boulevards . . . the windowpanes of paradise take a step forward, and the angel murmurs: *old desires will be extinguished,* then he fumbles in his skull and between his thighs . . . a pink razor blade, damp, a large bouquet of void and a budding gaze lashes at the blueness of the sky . . . boiling water bursts out laughing.

The bad taste of alcohol tingles of suns, speech roosting on its perch bit into a bad smell— gradually we became lost in the rain forest—between heaven and earth and time's tune.

Let's play something that isn't that sick . . . in a paradise parking lot we turned on rapping with angels . . . have you forgotten that you might smoke a little bit? . . . Echoes of silence, a legend as small as dawn . . . is my head a mattress that jostles every day? Is it a decoration crammed with perfect symmetries? . . . I have a lot to do and I will not try to get into your universe—a broken voice, like a dead man's, the robot's bla-bla ovation, a robot who meditates on the debris of his own art—don't listen, daylight is fading . . . the echo of the civilization of other people . . . we drink champagne or champagne and whiskey, I light my first cigarette, a danse macabre on the highway . . .

far off the world invents itself (and they never mention sleeping waters) sexual cameras explore time . . . Paris-Vagina, the universe of the very good is populated by the skinned alive (I think children are right to lie as they breathe, their fingers stretched in the dust, they know they weren't dreamed up) . . . *Up clear creek or anywhere else are never the same*—specters, illusions, day breaks swollen with blood, naked fountains spurting Zim Zum flowers and the heavy breath of darkness . . . death? A song entertains me away from it: WOPBOPALOOLOPBAMBOOM RUBBER SOUL . . . *I've got my mojo working* . . . A rhapsody of scented leaves . . . embolism-slogan . . . other births raining like the knell . . . we live in the same empty alley in the same heaven.

The earth will mourn the death of blue . . . all the trees are awakening, dawn registers its first message . . . for the best and the worst, we don't really know what the others said, or didn't say—the important thing is to be seen and heard among the stars with a thousand points on Piccadilly Circus, through the floods of neon lights of New York and Los Angeles—allow the moths in and get lost in the middle of Times Square . . . a blue star will alight on a water lily and birds will have a press conference . . . the glints of a virgin forest, nature babbles on the traces of the void in which we live, will we ever reach our destination?

The last roses are dying—and it all invents itself, revolutionizes, is created and unmade and bursts around the environment—in the hail the birches look like the recumbents guarding the entrance to the motionless village. God-skeletons irrigated by barbarity, target-zodiacs of images on a leash.

191

That's when the wind pulls away from the game.

Here, two centimeters away from the skull, we're transcended into horror and shit. The dialogue of spaces dies in the rainbow museum—makeup stabbed by a sigh—lights go out, Instamatic Kodak Polaroid Rolleiflex IBM Xerox in the journal of Margins and Herbariums . . . a twilight of spittle is broken on the waves . . . awful violence takes the place of liberty.

Secret militant bodyguards and the 3rd dimension rats sign our declarations of independence— forgers always answer—laughter spreads in time and space.

You should *come* into the world, avoid the slightest friction with those who look towards the past . . . you know that death has raised its fees . . . I talk about that often, *like that, in the air,* and it's raining everywhere else, it's raining on night's anvil.

DOOMSHOW—a green moon, millennium tears in the Yeti's eyes, God elbows his way into the machine room—echoes turned off in the foliage . . . A neon zoo, infinite-laser . . . there are still guys *leaving and returning* from Kathmandu . . . it's too late to answer you, too late, or too soon . . . *BREATH DEATH & KOZMIC KAPERS ABOVE ME,* flowery enigmas in the mummy's eyes . . . moths are playing dominos— blueberries have borrowed gold from the bows of light, *and I just fell back into my mind . . . DEATH WILL DRAFT YOU MOTHERFUCKERS!* Twilight wounds over the ruins, supernatural parking meters and stoplights of decapitated colors, evil machines, violence, attacked, death, death, *the word is DEAD*— Media Video in the streets of the world, *Learn Baby, Learn! . . .* the tall trees move and burn the games of solitaire, our roads cross and it isn't by chance . . . October Session, *the beat goes on, one more time C SHOOT THE NEON! SHOOT THE FUCKING NEON NOW! . . . whether the water is salty or fresh shit floats* . . . There is no one here . . . after the deluge? . . . *I check the time, it's fun & nada . . .* a lobster was licking the soles of my feet, seagulls were drinking skim milk, the cats translated Coca-Cola into Dutch—an imaginary hemorrhage on the pavements of London, creatures having descended from Olympia—garden-

side skulls, sexes under glass, handyman death . . .
missiles bark, the just fall, the others get up—despair
does gymnastics on the screen, silence has signed a
pact with neon, and neon with violence . . . a tear
erases not the shadow of a smile—snow imprisons the
wind and seduces wild honey . . . *Great Balls of Fire
For A Pornographic Budgie . . .*

Electric night in the lurch, the 33 record is
scratched, and then *the others* are left in the flames,
drinking blood, and the reality, unique, dead to the
world, and the poets' known affirmations, a soul for
me, fools! . . . never could read a single line, nor
remember a word, an image . . . cosmic snots cajoled
by the hicks of space, skulls trapped in porthole
sounds of *parking lots* sprinkled with blue roses—
action-images gas-stations puking hilarious stories . . .
blues are easily written and hold themselves back
because they are pure emotion . . . humid mists escape
from the guts of neon lights, and dawn against the
night in any country nailing sadness and melancholia
to the turquoise curtain that Cochise placed on the
horizon—crazy megapoles and atomic jukeboxes . . .

A busted moon smeared with night . . .

(Fate, said the poet who only has you . . .
talking just for talking that insurgency is a public
concert, beyond all fiction, rejecting demons, robots,
bad vibrations, *dibbuks*, allegorical violence . . . *fate
no one will answer) . . .* let the wild flowers dance as
well as the grass, the shadow-sound reaches the sea
and laughs at abysses . . . knock it off, poets! . . .
intrepid travelers stick to the wheels of void and life—a
deep turning—we're still on a background of night,
between *it exists* and *it doesn't exist* . . . we're still
embarrassed by silence and apocalyptic creakings—a
little bit of hell in these pages—and I vanish in the
arms of the wind, the customer is king, and God is
always right.

WAR . . . DEATH . . . THE RASH . . .

A door ajar (honeysuckle trembles) . . . a black
candle in vinegar . . . in clouds flesh stumbles . . . A
torrid Hit Parade, the sunflower dies in the Pop Music
arena—porcelain-slumber as light as foam enchants
the cats—war, death, curses—a broken dream enters
the lying thighs of the universe . . .

COSMIC Whore, Polaroid Blues . . . cities
shout and vomit heavy metal . . .

An extinguished flame under a lotus flower—a
hateful glance slips over our poor daydreams—a cop
goes by . . . a flood of debris and shit . . . cul-de-sac
vision . . . the sky dilates, and that *elsewhere* can still
enchant us . . . the Brain Police were born with that
cracking . . . sequences for *strobe poets*—we can say
anything now, particularly, the truth—night weeps
quietly, only the earth makes fists . . . at the bedside of
a cloud smoking blue pot to conjure the *politics* that
bore the galaxy.

Visa for a bone sky, the earth is emptying out

. . . silos of tears . . . war and peace . . . minaret-explosions . . . I embark on that fuse while God wastes His time doing crossword puzzles . . .

Sex-shards planted in neon . . .

Blue explosions in the pool halls of Assfuck City . . .

And behind the clouds trees sob in the golden twilight . . . dream-echo rising to the sky . . . I light another cigarette, the stars stumble . . .

Planet EARTH-GONG—

smoke vandalizes what I was going to say . . .

So many things happen—

so many words . . .

(And there are so many people who become real)

a handkerchief on the sea . . .

multicolored branch-visions—

fire provokes the mountains . . .

Sexual totems and the world empties out . . .

Sun-stripes over the industrial suburbs—a cramp wears a hole in the forest . . . flowers in the windows of the sky—our world forever irresolute, do you hear, you who were born adults? . . .

Irresolute, but all the way to the end described on the lining of silence.

THE ENEMY IS THE WORD

The enemy is the word.

Joe Staccato blinked in the metallic crackling welded to android haze that hangs over Miami Beach.

A spy's face screen, sex toys, a panoply of pitmen . . . Joe vanishes in the nucleus of night with no passion, clumsy and stupid . . . operation *"Love is the Law"*—living death in the dungeons of censorship—spies stuck to authentic monthly salaries of the Villains of Space . . . extremists disguised as Christmas trees, fat, paranoid cops, and all the people *self-made* (and whom we can't fool) . . . the Scandal kid, Joe Verminex, this is the mad hogs' times.

Operation *"I Play My Last Card"*—the extremely reduced appearance of the evening editions—heart-rending themes and social neuroses we can capture by chance with general information . . . themes that contain the tame signs of the living and the dead. Language frenzy. Images in six colors, coded and crossing the tantric puke of several generations . . .

Our instructions are compressed in the transitory sex of the law and order robot. The international assassin totally exploits the themes of love and social progress—like an idiot he was repatriated into the sexual and torrid afternoon of the coldest summer—those ladies mock us and it's really too bad, but let me smile when you speak about the sexual revolution—liberation movements are like so many cream tarts frustrated by the press . . . Suzy Creamcheese and Bébert Hallucinex track the hangers on in the porn movie houses of Piccadilly Circus and Las Vegas.

Joe Verminex is at the head of the pack, he

197

forgot his birth date in the post office box of the sexual proletariat, vanished during the showing of a horror film . . .

The enemy is everywhere, invisible, gray, sneaky, rapid, unbreakable, mixing everything up, conversations and rose perfumes, social neuroses and delirious interpretations . . . the dead are ambitious, like the old toothbrushes found in the crappers of Skid Row . . . obviously I think of all that along with marriage contracts, death certificates, secret reports, because the Wimpy Monkey ordered me to write another book—well, I'm bringing you along and give it to you at random—we talk day and night, worlds crack gently, sometimes the world trembles, and images hit one after the other by poets, don't sell at all. I'm pleased. What poem has lit up a head since? . . . for ever . . . none I suppose . . . the enemy is the word that survived—so, tough titty, *let's write* since the Wimpy Monkey wants us to and that he's ready to pay, what logic—And there are fools who say that when we get published we have a hand, an arm, two of them in the gears . . . assholes! . . . drift-cameras show you the way . . . you're the flat calm, you're the neutral objectives, you're the words and the images.

The enemy isn't Joe Staccato over Miami, they claim that in the nucleus "Love" Esperanza is stuck to the spy of space. Paranoid extremists. Operation *"More Fear Than Evil"* . . . And working hard the rabid hogs climb every social ladder . . . platitudes extremely reduced, caught by chance with the image- signs of six generations . . . the international idiot mocks you, that creamy hanger-on fiddles with Verminex's sex forgetting the unbreakable prole . . . . social neuroses to go . . . of course, another book, at random, let's talk earth, poets have survived on flat calm . . .

Gray but the word babbling—screen-face in a night without passion—*"The Law"*, a living dead man disguised as a tree, the people who hung onto the Scandal kid and Joe Operation . . . *"I Play With The Evening News,"* a little late though . . . general information going through codes and boiled instructtions . . . *law and order* in the afternoon, it's really too bad, Suzy Creamcheese's movements are our birth dates, sometimes invisible, ambitious conversations in the Monkey's crapper. Oh, with all that I take you away day and night beyond the worlds, with images puked by logic . . . happy, I guess—have what we write in our hands, a hand, an arm, neutral drifting you are the words.

Clumsy sexual mist and Joe vanishes in the censorship dungeon. Vicious fat cops work for the Ugly Organization, Verminex Hallucinex, international puke . . . operation *"Promiscuity Forbidden"* . . . I hear the ladies crack in Las Vegas, near my gray mail box, I sniff the perfume of roses and old toothbrushes— ordered me to write—feeble monkey . . . gently cracking the soft word . . . idiots in the gears . . . you're the images.

KRISHNA'S CRABS

Please, get Krishna's crabs out of my soul . . .
Please take your dirty socks off my heart, plus
your morbid political gadgets . . .
Please, don't invade my personal spaces . . .
I'm here for no one . . . fuck off! . . .
And, tell me who's fighting whom? And why?
The modesty of the social picture is found in
the underworld of society—I can't stand the smell of
laundry—what do you want? A molecular revolution in
Japanese sewers? The dirty dishes of the dead? . . .
your absence has nothing to do with science-fiction.

An energy crisis, a loss of speed and an
emotional question—please, get these gurus out of
here with their gray teeth, swamis and other cock-
suckers, get these inferior consciences out of here, get
these maniacs and CIA agents out of here too—may
the sound waves erase the stupid babbling of poets
who haven't entered the XXth century emotionally
yet—that's enough! . . . who's fighting whom? And
why?

Erase the cops, paranoid physicians, inform-
ers, Chiefs of State, philosophers allergic to life, errand
boys and pest dealers . . . erase the jerks, rats,
groupies, followers, erase the galaxy's dust . . .
Operation *"Ah Ah Ohoh Hihihi"*—I look elsewhere, I
trap the drawers and files of reality, I erase those who
were born adult, those who have grown up and seen
all, I erase heroes and molds, while I drum on the
napalm-sofa . . . All those who fall and can't get up, all
those who die on huge continents, all the generations
that will never be *normal,* both physically and
mentally—nothing to be done . . . audio-visual signals

and atrocity-smiles, a Western odor painted on the brain-prick . . . street language living and dead in a grimace. You're warned . . . a question of money, of course, and many other things.

Obsessive fear, sexual abstinence—disfigured on the screen you implore, "Valium, please! Valium!" . . . we finally leave the man's body only to lose our footing in a sign of life.

A marmalade of dawns cutting into the sky.

You, blue people, agonizing on the electrified railing, what have you got you say?. If only you had something to say! . . .

Legalized homicide at every level. It's free.

Joe Kick Sandoz walked on clouds with Sergeant Pepper, he watched the world turn, rising in the stratosphere . . . an ocean of music and peace, a blizzard of colors and pearls . . . violence stole from nerves, terrorizing intellectuals traveling on prick mobiles made of cream Swiss cheese—angels whistle that masturbation is the message, they whistle among the records of video-consciousness.

Zoom in the Sepia Kid's crotch.

Space riots.

A sexual safari in the desert of trash cans on episode-outskirts.

NEON level—tapes torturing history—sane reactions on the American side, the ideological haze of pure reason . . .

The conscience-riot in a contemporary *fix*— pathetic and comical at once . . . the curtain is rising, rats enter on stage with The Rainbow Girls . . . love-love, I've lost my San Francisco-o-O baggage . . . none of it was very photogenic . . . agitators are always ungracious.

Please, get lost and tell me who's the dealer

agonizing in the dish water?

Your absence comes at the end of this special edition . . . we find ourselves in the middle of a question . . . nubile swamis cruise in Dublin's YMCA halls.

Erase the cops and shut the others in allergic bubbles. Erase. Erase. I look elsewhere and I see you dying on the sofa, smiling, an odor of dead streets and state secrets . . .

"Give me the Valium . . . yeah, I'm nervous . . . I lost my footing in heaven . . ."

"You, Kleenex-people, what can I say to you?"

Spatial masturbation and bubble-gum-goulash . . .

Violence, violence, listen—please, please get rid of these evil air-waves—enough! . . . errand boys impose their mediocrity on this galaxy . . . A trapped opera, you'll see everything . . . continent-grimaces . . . Western-thing . . . are you following me? . . . those people, please, erase them—a lack of signs, blue obsessions . . . you say, it's all free?—you're cabbage in Swiss cheese, *mi amor* . . . a sexual zoom on a Pygmy's hemorrhoids . . . simoom wind in his crotch . . . history barks . . . prick mobiles and *dune buggies* terrorize tourists . . .

Krishna's crabs want to share the fruits of their experiences with the world. "Hare Krishna oyster faces!" . . . the modesty of an odor—an electric scream shatters the Commune of Infinite Love, "Get rid of those filthy dykes, emotionally erase those love-bugs" —And why? And why not? . . . "Fascists! Fascists!" reality's dealers have brought forth scabs, always a lack of money, and the police, of course . . . Joe Kick Sandoz cuts up dawn with a blowtorch, he's walking on a carpet of pearls, angels whistle at the Sepia Kid's multicolored records—episode-riots in American suburbs . . . then back to London in the purple fog . . . *the dirty dishes of the dead,* pure Vedanta in the crapper of a greedy West.

Please, do as the homeless do, do things like everyone else, jack off! . . .

"Have you taped what the western garbage disposal says?"

"Yes, and having said *that:* He who sells his mother loses his neurons . . ."

"Does he control your brain-mold?"

"Yes, and secret agents put crabs in my bowl of rice . . ."

"Do you have *written* pages within reach, and complete pages too?"

"Why?"

"I've got to get this fucking book moving forward . . . I've been fucked up enough by the sparkling turns of the pimps who claim to be publishers . . ."

To burst in a comic strip interrupted by reality, to never come down, never return, continue to soar with botched chromosomes and all the fried circuits—and what, what's the use?—I must sell them the great shudder, flamboyant anguish, *pistachio-nihil* and refined pleasures . . . *Om Om Ding Dong . . .* Vision hygiene, ecstasy, the morality of work . . . I hear them jostling in the jar, a psycho-social role for vegetarian hags and average cadres—I see nothing wrong with that—police skidding in the streets of Onan City . . . I've no idea how to resolve the problem of over-population, of pollution, of the nuclear danger, of inflation . . . I know a little about how to wipe my ass, I know how to roll my *joints,* that's all, don't give a fuck about the great social gestations . . . nature casts you into the world, life gives you to life, then by an order

204

from God it swallows you and shits you into space, squisssshhhhhhh!

Computers and their electronic tentacles take care of you, tele-guiding you into televised death—cosmic pork pâté, songs, electric chronicles, *Utopia Landing Module*, an infallible precision of words and images—an angel goes by, an orgasm cracks slowly under the rug . . . a pathetic festival! . . . Operation *"I Am A Fool But How Dare I Be So Handsome"* . . . Even if angels blow on your touristic equipment, setting fire to the Sacred Dildo will come to naught. Explore your own shits, smear yourselves with toe jam, limp with dirty briefs and the visiting cards on the suicidal mountain chains . . . the pink ego plays in the strategic choker, oh, no, guys you can't plant radishes by electrocuting the hag plugged into the empty cases of the catatonic hippie—fortunately there are thousands of hippies and yippies in civilian clothes...

"Sweet Jesus, Mrs. Jones, who would've thought . . ."

"Oh yes, such good manners, and always very clean, and an education . . ."

"Um, obviously we can all make mistakes . . ."

That's how the sausage-brain chooses, sorts out, controls and combines the most diverse information.

"A shot for the grandmother, two! We're going to inflate her needs . . ."

Nothing more is darkening the social horizons.

Crazy Blacks start interminable technical discussions, a strategy for sexual guerilla a warfare—strange conversations in sewers and sleazy bars—they age fast, a fifty-year-old parenthesis, it happens, cosmetic-brain doesn't answer anymore . . . cucumber-brain registers the moments of her survival . . .

Short-circuited shudders—a starring role in the can—social skidding, and nature shits on you, and you crack gently at advertising agencies . . . *"How dare I, Mrs. Jones?"* . . . a shot in exchange for your mother?—you can't sell Western garbage to just anybody.

And this fucking book that doesn't advance more than the others, anyway. I work for flamboyant pimps, for visionary bananas, and I'll have to pay to wipe my ass . . . *"To Be So Handsome,"* being obliged to obey—the electrocuted Dildo, oh yes, they never believed me, Mrs. Jones, never—dancing Blacks in Survival Street . . . forward men! For France! . . . I made myself play the part of the *Pistachio-Nihil* publisher . . . brain pollution—that's all, don't give a shit for social horizons . . . life offers you tentacles and pork pâté— leave that dirty underwear store . . . crabs and Hippies have vanished . . . An angel goes by, I hear it grumbling in this chronicle—*"I'm a fool but I know about refined pleasures"* . . . an orgasm shakes the mountain chain . . . a Hippie vanishes in civilian clothes in that cucumber-void.

Another shot and a skidding of ideas.

The dirty thing explodes in white jelly. Zero-Eternity. People talk. The world turns. A scream erases the fingerprints. Colors plunge into word-closets and break everything. People who write too much beat you up scientifically, a little sadness and two blistered fingers of goodbye. The stench of these millennia is still present, and Mrs. Jones says: "Good Lord! Why whip an Arab in heat, for that?" . . . Mrs. Jones the eyebrow licker vanished with Chopstick Charlie in a silent film in color.

Another shot—it's time to have a drink—it's time to collect a little information.

206

X IT'S BETTER THAN NO ONE

X ended up by being tired of being someone else and playing the role of no one. X laughs silently with insects licking every centimeter of fresh blood. X is always after an idea, having no prejudices, more or less maniacal. X controls his gestures, like a bleeding hog in his pink cellophane diver's suit. X takes sun baths and drinks gin and tonic. In Summer, for strange reasons, Whites detest the color of their skin.

Non-verbal communications and social pregnancies—computers and cameras think of you, *for you*, and, of course liberty of action isn't for every foreigner—pre-future caught among the financial pages, has already taken off from the technological chessboard that helps our sleep . . . that those who overflow with love may scratch their armpits . . . an eco-bucolic saga within everyone's reach . . . the last mystics roar quite powerless and peel off their faded disguises—puberty time rings in sexual factories, masses of mutants are carried away by an anti-cyclone of shit, a perverse opera and a universal cunt . . . each environment contains all information, no matter what the political regime is and the value of money . . . techniques for sale, ideological manipulations, process-and-produce controls—I don't divulge these messages for commercial gain . . .

Then the Mediocre Symphony bursts from sleeping mouths, hiccups, moans, pig grunts, farts, belches . . . thousands of idiots, stunned, crushed, invalid, deformed, mutilated, paralyzed, ravaged, horribly dead and alive—of course, I would like to talk about something else, say and write poems maybe, the way I used to do . . . I have just returned, from a rather long *trip,* a lucid flash back . . . but again images are consuming me, I don't give them any time of, thousands every day—those images burst every second, crossing space, jostling beings and things—neon-scissors, ready to cause the universe to burst, an electronic saga that gives you the freedom to interpret it any way at all. A few ambiguities, I agree, but how can we take sides if we want to express ourselves and communicate? . . . the machine has seized (maybe *accidentally)* power, the machine controls and destroys everything. A few personalities, totally autonomous are ready to leave this planet forever—the world turns, the global village explodes . . . typewriters and printers crackle, dance, smoke, hypersensitive, plugged into tape-recorders and TV sets, plunging flabbily into blue and pink horizons—coffee-break, a public menace buzzes, filthy, grotesque beings are guided by remote control to demonstrate—quite an appraisal, abominable hiccups, burned eyes, stoned skulls, massacres, echoes of worlds coughing in the morning fog . . . screams, prayers, supplications, howls, hymns, speeches, bazaar-prophecies, a thick flow of platitudes and absurdities . . . sleepless nights cut in half by police shards, spaces invaded by men bent on extermination.

The Summer of platitudes, we would like to be exceptions for skin reasons. Computers take off. Action—operetta-mystics in shit factories—the Opera of commercial ends, process-images of consumption—a smothering saga, rationed universe, zombies surface on the Ocean's shivery skin . . . Crazy Whites linger on the screen uninvited . . . non-verbal erections, a mutant's anterior existence is mixed up by the TV-chessboard, love, grimace and impotence—we're in the information mold . . . impotent poets are turned into cankers and insects, the artificial symphony of the prophecy—things burst under the sex scissors that leave you no way to communicate, I agree . . . the old swami is penitent because of his Brooklyn accent . . . scissor-things, plugged into every horizon, tragic demonstrations, worlds cough and melt on the shard-screen . . . an evangelical reality in the crapper at the Guys & Dolls . . . I hate the social color . . . puberty hour rings in the middle of chaotic mists vaporized by the anti-cyclone—sales and controls of sexy messages, images of hell torn apart cross my personal space—you may interpret this any way at all, but don't come near me, there are already quite a few who were unable to return . . . you follow me? You know what I mean, human brothers . . . that all loses balance in pink and blue . . . abominable menaces, say you—thick flows of conclusions and galactic hiccups.

AUTOMATIC PILOT

Claude Pelieu

SEQUENCE "FLASH"

The final flash will be presented in an underground *parking*.

We are what we don't know and what we don't think.

Shaw said that the most extreme form of censorship was assassination—The Himalaya of calumny or the head of a judge?—Here they don't rebel, they submit, sleep, live, die, and seagulls devour an old mattress, skeletal neon twinkles, here, no one waits for anyone or anything, they recoil, the arbitrary illuminates the time-interval . . . I'm alive, I'm writing this book to tell you that I'm alive, and so are you . . . red and blue vibrations against time's mirages.

Such and such, this and that.

Reality throws us back onto the sounds of chance.

Computers use our sounds. We flood the resonant structures.

LSD sequence, so as not to cry I decapitate and eviscerate my teddy bear . . . the sandwichman jacks off . . . inside/outside break ins . . . radio Gnome Flip-Flap, a wide door is about to open . . . we remember tomorrow as if it were yesterday.

Sequence abyss-photo—the simplest things mix with fiction—eroded wild mint, forget-me-nots erased by frost, landscapes and houses of cards, and the spontaneous song of waves, Frisco Bay in filigree as open as a sound . . . the electric mosaic of Penzance, St. Ives and the Los Angeles airport as open as noises crushing silence.

News terrifies, compromises, news spatters you, you can't react *personally*.

211

I don't read the newspapers. I don't touch crowds, I'm indifferent, uncommitted. God insists on silly songs . . . is that why every weekend is sad? (who wants to drag the sounds of this decade along?) . . . dancing matinees, distant pasty voices . . . flakes of men and landscapes, flakes of sex . . . volumes of unedited jungles . . . voice-explosions . . . high flames play on the walls . . . it's late, it's early . . . *what is it?* . . . this is what I see, and now I want to see something else. TV-Ass turns to stone.

A burn resembling a thud.

Dead and stiff on the highway, an old dog was still chewing gum . . . TV viewers are furious . . . video . . . shit-hole . . . a reunion of town councils, social problems, discussions . . . well it's the furthest from my thought, and I don't think I'm wrong . . . are you interested in knowing if I worry about refugees and if I consider that—I turn to stone too, and I hold my hands toward the flames that illuminate Uptight City, Dog town and Bottleneck Grove—we want to laugh, laugh to the end of the day with simple words like lightning, laugh about poets' prison life and commercial trips as prophesied . . . and, of course, for some, the last word for God—perhaps—anyway, there is nothing tragic in that.

To break the solitude of a mole hole-vision, strident hysteria, collective paranoia, insane grimaces, meaty-horizons, reality's phony vertigos spit in your faces, and the rats weep with emotion . . . we wait, we'll never stop waiting, fire between our shoulders . . . the canoe of emotion tips over . . . I swear that it will be colder tomorrow . . . also, I've never seen you! . . . bubbles hollowing life, and time—stereo world unclenches its teeth, gray death chews on a bubble—

I push mine along with a frozen crackle, I travel in the wind's outside pockets . . . Electric Zoo . . . a statue is shattered, an orgy of silence in the debris of time.

The Earth's spirit marks us with a swift line.

Festivals demolished by death thinking out loud. We're inside walls and nothing can take our place. West winds don't know where to put their laughter.

COCA NEON

Coca Neon, I've got those deep river blues.
Under the sand a tearful rose, *"Blue suede shoes, gorrillaman"*, and me, outside, *outside*, that's to say at 100 km/h, the wind is shooting arrows.

Neon strangles itself.
Flowers died on the mirror—we're in the wind's hands—we have no definitive goals and yet there are two small flowers in your eyes that mock the wind's haystacks.
Transistors, panoramas of consciousness, echo dust of the whole world, silent sparks green wood tortures your desires. In full sunlight, lying on colors, splashing the mirror, neon strangles itself. Violates silence and flees like a torpedo, a gust of *Cornflakes* smothers the sleepless night.

Neon-Gallows—scarlet cassettes cross the screen—thousands of tears overflow with the light, mouths palpitate like comic strips, a light voice made of milk and honey moves stones and color-sounds . . . the sun sat on a dolmen . . . compasses drown, and I'm dazzled, and I say to myself it's still yesterday—silence axes clocks, and fear harnessed to night bleeds a false note.
A glance on the bloody gloves of the Birdman, the planet's sexual fear is on the side of the political horror.
TV-Pork Chop, the breach is stained with dried brains—we're innocent—the fire's wrecked, the wind carries away our secret tears. TV closes its wings on the wild flowers.

215

The Death of the Great Spirit—poetry that must be, that is, that will be anything at all, and more, anybody in the singular/plural, a cabin in the sky . . . A century has gone by between our legs, in a tube of black light . . . the automatic pilot comes out of himself, and images scale someone else's consciousness.

Some visitor, some message.

Fuck the world! FUCK THE WORLD NOW! This is your last chance . . .

The sun revolves around a sad song—spray turns toxic behind that curtain of trees, the wind howls in the streets on fire . . . marsh-words, wounded bodies, separated from their souls . . . the heavens filled with screams, white rumors of apocalypse, and the wind dashes onto the rocks—the sea stirs its colors, the horizon's floating—those who predict stink, look! . . . a seagull's huge cry startles the photographer.

Coca Neon Polaroid Rainbow—the quivering moaning flesh of the rain forest moves people like a dog run over on the universe's dance floor—the hills sparkle, *"Blue Grass"*, rain has washed it all, the tide's ebbing, wind's rising—what happened? Nothing . . . nothing, no . . . really nothing . . . God has taken the habit of masturbating . . . here the threat of all writing, *literature,* a hideous effort, awful sadness, feeble magic—the landscape is a brazier, an echo of every language, and this continent is inhaled like a huge sob, chance lands on the back of a hand . . . bits of words . . . the sky trembles as soon as death plays with life, and in the dark flames bend like wild flowers, aware of what is happening to them, weren't able, like me, *to think* themselves dead.

Dawn is publishing this special edition, and

we spend our time sorting out bits of words.

Nerves torn by neon I'll have you know that smoke runs over this page.

What is deep in your eyes?

Nothing. I know it. I've received too many people influenced by fear.

Invisible tattoos, punches swollen with blood —it was the end of life—NEON WILL CRACK!!!

I see Warhol again caught between a yellow ticket and a forerunner sign, like a blood clot . . . this world is empty sometimes, and *popcorn* sings, the deaf have no modesty . . . water's sound flowing among fluorescent flowers, red lights drowned in *ginger ale*, and silver clouds—art gives you a little kick, *new art IS big business,* just remember that, look at Marilyn, an icon, in the firmament, lost, rolled around by mandibles made of Hollywood foam— Marilyn wanted to see the colors of her lips, and now in the *video-recording* sky the mourning of a smile . . .

A triple murder, a few rumors, a distressing suicide, two drowning on Fire Island . . . I hang on to the wind . . . false news licks the black and blue sky . . . the universe floats planting its pastel dyes on the reef-highway—rainy tickets exchanged for this discolored world—ten a.m., a flesh taxi explodes . . . the wind barred like a check by lightning and rain howling in the empty streets . . .

Brain Police! Zipper Puke! Coca Neon! The Next Flush! . . . a grenade of vitamins on the wrong side of *media video* spaces—the smell of snow dies out on a stone, mountains derail, and me and me and me . . . directed towards charm, horror, from silence to silence with the flowers.

It's not by chance that starving glances turn

into snow. Night is waning—cinéma-vérité of another age—a new kind of toothpaste, an electric banana, isolated tears are reborn in a dream.

The fire is dying—the bottles are empty—the cats don't recognize each other anymore, and that music announces something new, *tempest of flowers* . . .

The wind mistreats the head metal. Behind bars the soul starts a hunger strike—We might say to God: I don't love you, *I prefer you*—winter vacations for the shadow sounds . . . we're safe and sound, we find ourselves again in the ogive-skulls of launching pads, with passing reflections, lamp-stars, silken images . . . what are the stakes of your death?

Morning Song, morning evening, thanks again home-galaxy . . . snow inhaling all the colors of illuminated journals . . . nights ravaged by frost, indelible dialogues of rain and fair weather—and me, in a forest of sounds and images, *popcorn & spastic bananas* . . . the universe is a fried egg—dead birds carry the last echoes away.

Every day the *dead* idea kills real *life,* bubbles dominate actuality, flux and reflux—they're repainting trash cans of history at minimum, they swallow the sky's jacks.

What to do this morning?

Cut some wood, roll a few cigarettes, refuse to be wrong, to be right, not to be bored stiff, jump into a plane.

What can we do in a bread crumb sky?

The flowers are breaking apart. Eyes full of love vanish without crying to be careful. Landscape-faces in American colors—when all goes well tomorrow daylight will come—bachelor sun digs forever, we settle down in heaven very quickly . . . are those people stretched out on cold metal doomed? . . . see, a forgetful Ocean, savage, realistic, sweeps away the vanity of chatter . . . there are very few *words* capable of resisting the powerful vacuum of chit chat . . . we absorb ourselves freely as we plant our laughter on the window panes. Musical comedy of the elusive *Belle Époque*. Instinctively we go towards the meaning of revolt—we're abandoned, our backs to the wall, we went by too fast, without realizing that the air and foam circulate with intrepid travelers . . . well, it's not the right time to hit on my *marshmallow* . . . there's nothing to say, we're in front of the Sperm Bank, a zest of a grimace occupies the world.

Beauty institutions are on fire.

And you, pygmies, arrive too late, with old addresses and bad vibrations.

Cameras rush into the darkness and give themselves to computers.

Lovely off-handedness taking the word to throw shit at the media allowing the green planet's colors to escape.

The war industry and techno structures of violence spit a bit of vomit—to be continued is the password of every author at the same publisher's place—later a rainbow of me so as not to live in a whisper, one dies howling and drinking ink . . . *death is our business, and business is good* . . . do you hear, you wild civilized creeps, a vision has no opinions . . . you will never be poets—sound-effect children, phosphorescent wrinkles—the Cartesian ectoplasm has gone by, the man without a country has shit in his pants, *ex-nihil* cleaner than a drop of napalm . . . superjerks enter the fifth dimension . . . robots gesticulate in neon reflections . . . airports surrounded by darkness . . . people always live hanging onto death.

We're here, nowhere at the boiling point, at their rope's end, we're bursting for the greater good of a piranha humanity . . . We're here, in streets that used to be full of people we don't mention them anymore . . . we split in neon and we're stronger than Xerox and IBM, but we can't store the flood of information manipulated by the hideous jaws of reality.

Snow buries silence.

Diagram Planet, photo sphere. In heaven trees stroll around and the rain sings, laden with shadows— the sun rises over a pile of dirty laundry, a fibrous break goes out with a bit of time—a flowers covers the screen, death buzzes and makes language inarticulate . . . we vanish leaving no traces . . . the fauna of space vaporizes lethal gases. Imagination shits in a strangely true note. Cavemen militants flip out. They were unable to break the barriers of the head with sexy grass. There are some *revolts that are allowed* and you mouth waters. *Hare Krishna Scumbags! . . .* Shut up! You're not even in the furthest universes of the brain . . . memories speak more softly . . . robots and *diskjockeys* don't remember in the same way . . . a fluorescent index searches through a lapping of muscles . . . the third eye, and one out of three adults in England has no more teeth—a paranoid crackling, hysteria, evil lighting— we're on board the *Sperm ship*, images scream in the dark, crammed into a grenade of rain.

A scream tears the earth apart, broken images, death recoils. A scream and the blue monkey penetrates another body, engraving the word *illness* on the end of a blackened spoon. A scream, rush hour

of the hero-ember agony, and a sad song stuck onto
the shadows . . . *Memphis Blues*, Sweet Jane in the
bayous of Louisiana—an ancient voice bitten by the
fruits of insomnia—twilight, a branchless night
crushes the cliffs of flesh, an explosion full of frost, and
dawn once again . . . icebergs changed into hands,
telephones lost at sea . . . Hamburger planet cracks
and breaks the windows—neon waves its black flag—
my hurricane-lamp looks nice . . . I'm here, I was there,
elsewhere nowhere . . . Maryland, New York, Los
Angeles, San Fran, London, Paris, who cares? . . .
infinity doesn't cause death to overflow.

Fear, drifting, fresh paint on the fat balls of actuality . . . via satellite in the golden dawn vandalized by a generation of piranhas who have taken on a *hip* air to excuse themselves . . . the magic conception of a given world, in spite of everything, seems to win over the *scientific* conception of criminals who crowd this planet—everything is obviously dumb—the myth of the machine, metaphysical dimensions, managed societies, ideological services, *avant-garde art* etc. . . . chicken shit submerges innocence . . . deprostrated poeticiens speak to us of primitive mentality, socialism, wild thoughts, the infinite trash . . . robots and the fuzz are at our service day and night . . . total war, racial, religious, planetary . . . psychedelic genocide, ecological genocide, electronic genocide—we may be the only ones who don't want to impose another way of life on others, let's leave that business to the baboons of the Fourth Dimension . . . worlds will be neither better nor worse, but surely different, livable . . . there are no words to describe those bewitching spells . . .

Infraction-life, boa-desire, laughter, grab bags . . . We've seen the sun's flowers . . . God sips the spinal fluid of His electors in the videos of the Universe—we're here, where we can breathe, inside and outside—we're here nowhere overall the landscapes, electrified thistles sign the light.

It was through icy knives of the Lower East Side, and we made the flowers dance—Death TV's antennae sucked the sky—conscience/comet and a sexy message on the arm of a shooting star . . . the wind made the lines in a hand . . . dawn, dead-water, rain, old photos splash the clouds, those dawn drowned people.

So well *so that* earth blue and scarlet silence—skipping words so well that *so that*—tension on every air-wave, screen-dog, SOS OD, Billy the Moccasin and Long John Silver killed an Indian for Nixon . . . a vaudeville of mouths and micro-taxis . . . chipped peninsula, wog neon, poisoned antennae and electric Camembert . . . laughter is reality, touristic comic strips, bites, Vietnamese streets of the planetary suburb, mad men and amnesiac bananas, cold brings a dead image back to you . . . a rainbow in that flesh store . . . events ending up in catastrophe, made into an image by the *pancake-landscape*—ossuary-sauna tattooed by rain.

God has no lips, snow is always dirty . . . barricades of words, *hot fudge sundaes,* balls with a view of the mother—have I been heard clearly? —hallucinatory images will bear the skin of beautiful language—here's the man who is astonished by silence . . . images ambushed in sewers, equinoxes of filth, a tidal wave of shit, super-jacked off cucumbers, candid cannibals gorged with effort . . . one day God created Switzerland, then Belgium, you know the rest . . . had to allow us to exist—the sun's prick bashed in the window, the psychedelic melon made its entrance into the universe, *Hare Krishna, knot-head!* . . .

Well, I do remember a quick trip in France . . . discovering the sweat of the 60s, erected into a cultural spire, *popcorn underground,* cream tarts, imported *dropouts* . . . "You'll see when you grow up", well, now we're grown up . . . have you seen something? Or someone? . . . amoebas howl with joy . . . Old Westerns and songs, sexual doodling, odor-plan . . . scissor-waves spit fire—what misery!—*death is crouched motionless in the middle of shit . . .*[1] Let's allow the dibbuks to invade our souls . . . visions, puzzles, vacations . . . not to mince our words . . . the *Tierce* of the century, the Festival of Squares . . . that's how we sacrifice certain *principles* profiting efficiency . . . ecological activity in crappers—who succumbs to charm these days? . . . The Universe loses weight, colors devour LP-smiles—a little sun on the sand, a few commas to displace, a coded message, a good contact, and the war is over. . . .

Life is empty.
The street is empty.
Odor-show. Socio-bah! . . . photos drowned in time's *lightshows* . . . life's a street, life's death-odor, *Zodiac Punk . . .* a corolla-mouth, and a hideous voice on the night-road imitating a real noise, *bossa nada, bamba mambo . . .* On the back of the ocean snow sings, a block of live flesh sodomizes the window of language—a wild cat growls on the edge of the path—an unreal scream jostles the airwaves. And once again void makes a paragraph.

Wrinkles and foreskins on the calendar—we made this night—militants enter on all fours into the crappers of history grunting like pigs.

I put all that on the tab poetry owes me, nana scratch, stupidity, simile-mourner, show and gut, an ideological hangover, throngs molded into the spectacle—alarm-man evicted from heaven, the voids of a cold summer still ring—a savage cry swallows heather . . . *media-visions,* ageless suburbs . . . I fall asleep on the tracings of every landscape.

---

[1]Georges Lapassade

The roses survive the first frost. Grass trembles on the top of the hill with cradle-clouds. Disemboweled dawn, dynamo-sex, the immensity of it changes skin—and you, dealers of changes of life—rain strolls around crushing a generation, the other one . . . cramps puking a little green smoke over Heathrow Airport . . . the jumbo jet takes off . . . London-NY non-stop . . . the control tower vacillates . . . the jet disappears in the blue night.

Snow, crystal, elastic islands. Whiskey, cigarettes, old Westerns . . . wind and dust carry the javelins away and millions of stars escape over New York City . . . the velvet back of silence . . . a stolen instant puts on an air of passing-time, light beats us up.

FLAKES OF FEAR

Space, listening post, blue song, an ever-missed meeting, drunkenness. The bursting of myriad skulls. The great shudder drinks something other than water. Pebbles throw themselves into the sea-blackened cliffs, stars and missiles like us submitting to inferior values—the West winds decapitate sand to defend themselves, and muscles with a bone base cut the skin-linen.

Masters and slaves, assholes at half north/south, never east/west, excluded with patriotic passions and season mourners . . . the cosmic underworld seizes the Grimace Galaxy . . . sparks put on their seven league boots, speed exploits their findings, nerves are happy to flee, pricks pointing forward.

Flakes of fear, fear hemorrhages—screens crackle, a collision of pink waves, giant dominos cross the field of echo-claws—minarets, merry-go-rounds, decals, geysers of laughter-light, gobbledy gook-Wog, erasures, we're on the chain hi-fi of eternity. And it's electrified! . . . televised wind blows from the Great Wall of China . . . wrinkled jungles . . . morning dew seduces a cargo of buckwheat . . . by the way, tell me, are you at ease with people who know what they want? (Those whose ideas never change) . . . I'm in the Arab-echo of the motionless village—I hear the sea—the moon crosses outside the crosswalk, fire on snow works unawares, crazy blacks cry: *Shake the Pumpkin, Baby! Shake! Shake!* . . . Today's already yesterday, *and the beat goes on, the beat goes on and on!* . . . megafuck! Shit! Groovy! . . . *shake! Shake! SHAKE!* . . .

So there—a movement of the crowd, an attack, an electoral season, a few troubles here and there, subjects we absolutely don't want to talk about, the end or the beginning of a war, for example the ugliness of the IRA or Vietnam, booby trapped letters, the taking of hostages, the bursts of machine guns and the bombs . . . all that's unimportant, *all that didn't* make the history of a Spring . . . and yet the facts, but *what facts? . . .* no one will have excuses for your freedom, your indifference, those facts have excluded us from history, and we throw ourselves into the pre-future, and you sit there on your asses, bloated with mediocrity. Barricades of cucumbers where heroes die, ruminating on their foreskins—signals of a little smoke here and there, they claim that there isn't enough nature for everyone . . . and the sexual proletariat unclogs into murmured time . . . fire tears the blue jungles, televised news doesn't tell you anything at all, disease spreads over the global village . . . no illusions when words are concerned, you'll continue to write, write to each other, without crying out, in French superwog negotiations, like pygmies, well it ain't my affair . . . all is unwinding, and so much the better . . . it's all turning into slobber, into rancid come, and colors shit language—sometimes the wind eats thunder, its song possesses all that it represents. Reality moves or it doesn't move. A mentholated shock, a draft of air—silence refuses to nourish the survivors, the murmur of the morning dew lives truth like a passion, the rest is unimportant. . .

For a long time silence has left the desperate and stupid tropical slowness. We're illuminated from inside. We're plowing fields of waves. Shoulder and casting away those who refuse to freeze in the veins of someone else, quickly, a drama with nothing and no

one, where we can hear the colors . . . *Full Tilt Boogie*
. . . Your censorship has had no effect, it will never
clear the silence that lives in us—Factual comic strips
and video lines against pathology and politics, against
cultural narks . . . all that will only last an instant op-op
frozen, congealed—audiovisual solitude, a green glint
cuts into the sky, a great white streak of lightning, and
the film unrolls—the studio explodes, then all the
lights go out . . . three or four dimensions to mix
people up . . . a sound of water in the pipes of time.

The swami has vomited his hamburger that
he'd eaten the day before, on the sly.

Sexy messages at auction on TV-ass. Porn
photos pinned onto every lip.

Belotte players disappear with strands of red
hot iron and blue waves in front of the Sky Bank.

A diffused message in every language: *we'll
be free when we'll be rich, rich and free, free and rich,
we'll be rich when we're free, free and rich . . .*

Violated neon . . . the wind's knives puke your
howls, starving brain techniques by the city-sounds . . .
Riots in the tubes of time.

Transistorized nipples, imagery-bodies, trem-
bling the waves disperse—death live on the screen,
North Carolina collage—crazy Blacks jack off furiously
onto the windshield . . . empty clothing abandoned . . .
even the headlines of daily newspapers have lost their
power, no one was able to do away with violence . . .
soon the milkman will deliver the paper in a cassette,
and the big green snake will play the flute—the
televised flash breaks down every barrier, we're born
with commercials and comic strips—and sometimes
the shadow of indifference is like the rain, a huge fist.

THE COLD BANK

Ray was in the hollow of a wave.

He didn't believe in his electric identity.

And I start again with images, for you, for you only—an amputated typewriter—a splash of color, screeching in time, non-color of neon-fever heated by French or American or Chinese gangrene, Arab or Russian (who cares?) cascades of urinals, the black years pushed into bones and voices . . . "death to jerks!", "vive peanut butter!" . . . and then oh oh arrrggh! . . . I awoke unsticking myself from the waterfall . . . "Death to bastards!" . . . and you assholes that I shit on the molecular scales, from one end to the other, shit-talk, combustible what the hell, assholes, you know what I'm saying and you follow me, satellites, tentacles, radars, sonars, towing seven million men—a mad computer skins your cortex, and then it's Summer, holidays in Florida . . . aspens here, silver poplars, birches . . . a blooming rose, the landscape lights up, the setting sun licks the horizon— warm postcards hanging onto *the spirit of the earth* . . . we roar with laughter along with flowers cut in drinking and eating, the piss-shit, silence tears the waves over Silver Creek, the wind carries away the most ordinary images, the wind doesn't have to worry about neighbors—I jotted that down on a patch of ferns, charms rush into it, spraying like fountains with extra-sensitive waves . . . Snow Hill, Primrose Hill, Hamburger Hill, Electric Rainbow Hill, and further on the hills of San Francisco, San Fernando Valley . . . fast we traveled like traces, *fast,* but how can we really remember? no one knows how memory really works—skies lined with honey asleep in the hollow of a cassette, films and magnetic tapes salivate when dawn comes assembling us at equal distances apart, the wind blows and gives a little light, eyes beg for a little warmth—we aim at the heart, the head, the belly . . . secret cries, laughter, pornographic pages and collages say we are right, expressing themselves with meaning and then turning to dust before our eyes.

Celluloid Coca Neon. Idiotic songs. Swells of known and unknown faces. Black gelatin trembling on the Jewish screen. Cowboys, *surfers*, bacteria, viruses, specters . . . the poet folds his vertigos and his angers like any other baggage, waiting for the invisible invasion, sitting on black hawthorns near electric fountains forcing the turquoise curtain of New Mexico to open, contemplating neon in the water, or the flowers . . . the rescue of mandalas melting in time and space . . . in these broken lines we have seen thousands of gods, planets born in water, pyramids of polyester clouds—emotion is great as soon as an angel is forgotten . . . thousands of postcards clear my eyes . . . we're always absent or present, that's why certain people call God *Mr. Everybody* . . . present, absent, violent, peaceful—electric signs, and neon-flesh, moons diffusing blue . . . once again I overflow towards the West.

The thousand-petalled lotus, tantric incantations and cut/ups mixing with the third spirit—the knots in the image pierce the fog—insomnia on the Cotton Roof . . . dreams, rags of dreams murmuring to the drowned men marked by dawn . . . the sun revolves around your destiny, meat at rest winks at the Yeti, voices abandon you here.

Look at daylight falling into a thimble, daylight makes a suffocating sound.

Distant lips. Ashy stars.

The air buzzes, Dead moons. Horizon-smiles.

The man gets out of the sand, the grace of grass inspires the wind—the weather is fine and the cats are on their way to the river—I'm in the hollow of a wave . . . my book is making progress.

Setting sun tears at waves and charms.

How fast do traces work?

Dawn-cassettes and dust-collages.

God *Mr. All Blue* . . .

Silver Creek, July-August 197...?—idiotic music—San Francisco, how can we remember? A film-memory expresses Coca cowboy and clears insomnia.

Falling . . . getting up . . . coming, going . . . seven billion men caught in a post card . . . to laugh and shit in silence . . . to piss on one's neighbors. Pornographic pages wink at pink sounds . . .

The show is dead. News riddles our environments of sexy messages.

Flipped out minorities don't know how to pick the messages . . . crazy Blacks go from hand to hand . . . Listen to the wild bulldozers bust genetic memory . . . between two sighs folded in the thick silence computers engulf the planet . . . crazy Blacks set fire to themselves in front of the Cold Bank.

ENTERING AND LEAVING

Silence, immobility, animals and machines . . .
We're on that electrified railing, a long time ago,
hanging onto a pasty grimace. People were strolling
around, avoiding the nuances of time's airs. Absorbent
gray waved in streets swallowed in light. Some
thought that that ambiance could be built among the
lines of a story—public taste right in the sky, proving
the existence of reality, holidays and the world
stretches out—death at will here and there, mocking
the thinness of public opinion. There's nothing new in
that.

(Here) some beautiful modern villas, luxurious,
integrated into the landscape, spacious bungalows
overlooking the sea, it all sparkles over the sunlit
sprays. Robots insist on expressing themselves in
millions of tons of TNT. Everything evaporates, opens
up, closes down, dies, rots, the worst lies travel around
the world at the speed of light, and we advance, going
backwards, burning our voices, barely furnishing
space and time.

The message diffused before the arrival of the
Villains of Space, even before the coming of the
psychedelic Fascism was: RESISTED, SUBSISTED,
SURVIVED, ENTERED AND LEFT. To survive, dead or
alive in front or behind the scenery—crossing walls
bunkers fogs launching pads, screens and dangerous
areas—a precise yet rainy technique. Who is *who*
among these broken lines engulfed by the event,
disappearing in pink sand?

CAMERA season—we don't systematically
take the side of violence and chaos . . . we refuse to
compromise ourselves with those marriage proposals

—a little creaky salute awaited its time in the mugginess of a July evening.

Those CIA agents were also colonels.

Heavy, damning files, hashed and rehashed by seditious conspirators.

Colonel Verminex, we don't have much to talk about anymore."

"Very well . . . we'll see each other in Polynesia."

"Watch out, don't fall into the sink."

So, chatting, slobbering, telling a completely fictitious story invented by informers and agitators, supervised by Joe Verminex . . . a report of crises that get along well with the police . . . a dive into the darkness of time, psychedelic Fascism, macrobiotic eloquence and the congealed left-overs of a counter-culture that doesn't dare give its name—the trembling fingers of those who have never come down, dying on this mosaic—we'll never talk about it again, superstars can't go backwards, already in a pasty way, the past has absorbed them.

The world's taste spreads all over. Water and spray here as well as words. Fear is evident on these pages. Lies ventilated by the ideological services in space. And behind the scenery, or in front of it, tatters of seasons and silence-cameras. CIA in the sink. An orange evening party and meringue-hashish, with trembling fingers to go backward and never talk about it again. Everything is ready. Faded stars in the sky. Here, modern villas overlooking the sink. Robots go around the earth, broken technique of a voice mixed with the fetid breath of the conspiring colonels and the secret agents, char women and *superstars.* I'll see you facing the darkness of time, in police glue . . . is that clear? An appointment in the nevermore evidence.

Reality, *we're only in it for the money, sap!*—
scintillating procedures of the four seasons on
holiday—we're advancing with the survivors. A rainy
Death in the sleeping waters. Words jump . . .
circumstances bringing bad omens . . . the story?
(conspirators, agitators, hitmen, commandos, mili-
tants, policemen, scapegoats, innocent passers-by,
marriage proposals economically evacuated through
the curtain of zippers)—fights in the empty streets,
crossing time on the first day of vacation.

"Don't fall into that mosaic of screams."

A blue flash erasing the card players.

Workmen come and go, menacing with their
jackhammers. They're handymen. Cameras in a state
of alert—troubling attacks, horrible and stupid—the
eloquent silence of the authorities. Flexible colors
crying out your names, soliciting the troubled gazes of
the spectators.

"Nothing will change the essential informa-
tion . . ." a meticulous relation to the facts erases all the
paranoias, the time tune disappears with precise
dates, with the debris of bad memories, the good ones
too, brain mush and a risky situation . . . an old poet
gesticulates, mumbling, grotesque and pathetic in the
broken light . . . sad, infinitely sad, lyrical clown
subjected to such imperatives? The bad treatment of
posterity whistling in the sepia dawn, *noblesse oblige*
was the password.

The man in gray dissolves in a suitcase,
unaware of the suffering and the overheated schedule.

Negatives of truth in the Chinese restaurant.
Absent customers vanish in the rowing-in-the-past
pain—streets paved in sexual hunger, finger tips
surfacing in the gutters—an *uptown* cry tears at the
reporter's shivery film. Sadness weaving tormented

sounds. Threatening crabs sucking at the sharp pains of a flip-flap generation. Psychedelic cops shining through the blade-ripped screen. *L'Année de la Fourchette*, do you remember? . . . they'd photographed that bloody, horrible crack and carved on her chest the word *WAR*, causing her brain to splash onto the walls of the kitchen, drinking her blood, skinning her spouse in the swimming pool . . . Fascist rustling in the heart of the unforgettable night, on the way to heaven, Operation *"Burnt Bread"* —another collage of scraps already bursting apart in the recent past, flesh-clots chopped by Joe Verminex and his disciples, sniffing garbage and toilet water, robbing medicine cabinets.

"We'll find each other again in empty eyes, darling . . ."

"Or in accidental surprises, my love . . ."

On the side of televised hip comedy nothing to tell. A patriotic walk of the conspirators.

There was a purple fog over Miami Beach.

"There isn't only the sea," murmured the conspirator, "there are mountains too."

We're sitting on police glue. People were wandering through reality, absorbing death, wavering like cops evacuated by the pipeline of time, crossing that mosaic of spray-cameras, impaling themselves on jackhammers of worker-agents . . . risky messages in the light . . . to survive in a macrobiotic night, naked, dying in the taste of the world, flying over the scenery, crawling among technical lines—yes-yes superstar yes-yes leaning over the sink, vomiting the latest information.

In time and space . . . *Tutti-fruitti* in the empty streets . . . Irving Rosenberg, the Ugly, right in the sky dragging the Red Dykes along . . . to express oneself in

238

the arrival psychedelics, psychic experience before or behind the purple lines of violence—CIA season and trembling fingers on the mosaic—Lee dies in Ray's backward walk, with orange tatters that were ready to talk. Pasty grimaces over New York. Gray landscapes lasting in space.

I cross the scenery, precise, rainy, a little drunk, displaced in the lines by the event, refusing the raspy salvation of the environment—heavy files, proofs to compromise Joe Veminex . . . the eloquence of the police? A dive into the sink so as never to return. Fear behind the silence-CIA, is that clear? . . . an appointment at the end of that process in sleeping water, with the innocent conspirators controlled by the psychedelic Fascist sounds—and the point in a few seconds . . . the curtain of zippers calming the savage outcries of the policemen, a flash on the state of alert . . . nothing will change *noblesse oblige,* trash in a suitcase, pain-truth surfaces with the shivery files and crabs . . . Joe de la Fourchette skinning Miami Beach.

Police-glue, I tell you, reality carrying empty-ness around, mosaic-colors breaking the cameras. Sexual hunger in the blade-dawn, street riots, savage police charges, the word WAR cuts through the passers-by. A re-splicing is advised. Fog murmurs.

The night of time and the evidence. We're going forward. Words jump. The players are erased. A troublesome silence in the crappers at the Miraflores. Precise facts pushed away by essential things. Sadness throughout the screen. Memories carves all around the swimming pool, tattered memories, dangerous operations in the past . . . trembling flesh in the empty eyes of secret agents . . . a televised comedy for the image hunter. The image consumer puts the fecal happening in place. *The Time-Eating Phallus, the*

Ejectable Vulva. The Radioactive Asshole, the Evil Gadget, the Masked Lobster and His Retarded Group, all those agents have caused the "utopian" virus to appear, that literary drama of political information, fiction and global vision compressed by the *mass media.*

Someone somewhere, and what happens, what doesn't happen . . . uncertain times . . . Amphetamine Cowboy, a stranger who doesn't stick to the image of the man he sees on TV . . . Psycho vision in the Molecular Studios . . .

The Red Bar is invaded by a horrible smell . . . every moment crushed by the hideous crowd . . . chance maybe, certainly reality . . . silence never announces the color images lost as the days go by the evanescent charms of culture, and the old poets in rags emerge, consenting victims of a feeble folklore, shit! Will have to shit somewhere very very soon . . . we use rare words, events bring eyes to the nuclear bordello, robots babble, salivating with moving stains . . . it's raining on neon lights, blue animals slip without a sound.

I don't want to meddle with the transistors of others. I forget what the folkloric colors are. Postcards agonize in the grass—dust and sobs, cries and flashes, dreams intercepted by neon-sounds—(another system, impossible to evaluate what is overwhelming the world) . . . a total lack of depth and psychology . . . Viruses and miasmas take hold of the streets, historians are grafted onto disease . . . what elements are you using now?

August 1973
UK. USA.

www.ingramcontent.com/pod-product-compliance
Lightning Source LLC
Chambersburg PA
CBHW060915250626
47159CB00008B/3015